Ruthless Choices

Heidi Stark

This is a reminder to never settle.

To remember that you deserve respect and kindness and love.

To remind you to hold those close to you who prove over and over again how much they care, even when your actions might cause them frustration.

And to trust your gut. It's rarely wrong.

If you or someone you know is experiencing domestic violence and needs support, please call 1-800-799-7233. If you are unable to speak safely, visit or text LOVEIS to 1-866-331-9474.

This is a dark tale with imperfect characters and impossible choices.

It includes elements of physical and verbal abuse, domestic violence, dubcon/non-con, rape and sexual assault, as well as elements of horror including gore and cannibalism. It also includes graphic sex scenes, including MF, FF and FFM.

Contents

1. Chapter One — 1

2. Chapter Two — 17

3. Chapter Three — 39

4. Chapter Four — 47

5. Chapter Five — 55

6. Chapter Six — 61

7. Chapter Seven — 65

8. Chapter Eight — 69

9. Chapter Nine — 89

10. Chapter Ten — 94

11. Chapter Eleven — 98

12. Chapter Twelve — 102

13. Chapter Thirteen — 109

14. Chapter Fourteen — 111

15. Chapter Fifteen — 120

16. Chapter Sixteen — 123

17. Chapter Seventeen — 136

18. Chapter Eighteen — 143

19. Chapter Nineteen   145

20. Chapter Twenty   151

21. Chapter Twenty-One   158

22. Chapter Twenty-Two   163

23. Chapter Twenty-Three   165

24. Chapter Twenty-Four   168

25. Chapter Twenty-Five   171

26. Chapter Twenty-Six   173

27. Chapter Twenty-Seven   176

28. Chapter Twenty-Eight   178

29. Chapter Twenty-Nine   181

30. Chapter Thirty   184

31. Chapter Thirty-One   186

32. Chapter Thirty-Two   190

33. Chapter Thirty-Three   192

34. Chapter Thirty-Four   195

35. Chapter Thirty-Five   200

36. Chapter Thirty-Six   201

37. Chapter Thirty-Seven   207

38. Chapter Thirty-Eight   208

39. Epilogue   212

Also By   218

About Heidi Stark   220

Chapter One

T he Past

Ruby

"Get the fuck off me! You're hurting me!"

I try to wrench my hand free, but his grip is too strong and I only anger him further. He increases the pressure on my wrist, growling at me as I feel the crunch of my bones beneath his huge palm. The man is nearly twice my size, and that extends to his giant hands.

"Stop trying to run away, you stupid bitch!" he screams. "You'll only make things worse for yourself! I need to teach you a fucking lesson!" Spittle flies from his mouth as he continues to howl at me, some landing on my cheek and adding insult to injury.

"Fuck you! Let me go!" I scream back, and in desperation, I attempt to knee him in the groin as hard as I can. I miss his crotch, instead merely grazing one of his massive thighs, but it distracts him for a moment and he briefly glances down. Once again, I try to yank myself free, this time twisting my wrist at an uncomfortable angle to make it as small as possible within his tight grasp. This time, I manage to slip out of his hold and back away in the direction of the door. My ankle turns awkwardly, and I yelp as I try to keep myself upright.

He lunges toward me and pulls me back toward him, his nostrils flaring with rage and his eyes glimmering with fury. His firm grip encircles my right bicep, his fingers pressing into the flesh so tightly I have no doubt he'll leave a handprint bruise.

I still don't know what I did to make him this angry. But then again, I rarely do.

"Don't try me, you stupid whore!" he screams. "I don't need you of all people giving me lip. Who the fuck do you think you are?!" He rears his free hand back to form a fist, and then hurtles it forward and smashes me right in the side of my mouth. Stars explode in my vision as my head snaps back and to the side from the momentum, my teeth jingling in my jaw, and I immediately taste copper.

"Please stop! You've made me bleed." I plead, as blood trickles from my mouth and down my chin to back up my claim. He's easier to convince when there's physical evidence, even though sometimes he'll refuse to acknowledge it.

I wonder if I still have all of my teeth, but I can worry about that later. If I make it out of here. I don't dare to wipe away the coppery red goop. Maybe the sight of my blood will snap him out of it and make him realize he's gone too far this time.

"Shut the fuck up!" he snarls. His eyes flash dark with rage, and his features are hard to recognize compared to the handsome, calm facade of a young man he shows the rest of the world. He saves this facial expression for me, and the occasional person who accidentally bumps into him on the street. To everyone else, he's calm, cool and collected at all times. "You're the one who put yourself in this position. You're making me do this!"

Letting go of my forearm for a moment, he reaches toward my shoulders and shoves me with all his strength, and I fly through the air as if I weigh no more than a feather. My body smashes against the bedroom wall before I land awkwardly on my tailbone on the hardwood floor. My head careens back and smacks hard against the wall, and my vision goes completely black for a second before bright white stars explode in my periphery.

I look up at him from where I lay slumped against the side of the room and my vision is blurry, only emphasizing his furious expression and serving to make his features look more warped and grotesque. My head is ringing from the impact, and my mind is focused on the sharp ache in my tailbone. I try to push myself up, but I put too much weight on my ankle too quickly and pain shoots up my leg, and I slump back down while I try to figure out how to stand.

He's continuing to yell, but I can't quite make out his words. It doesn't really matter what he's saying, anyway. The message is loud and clear. I have made him displeased, and I will never be good enough.

Maybe he'll leave me alone now that he's got me on the ground. Sometimes this is enough to get whatever it is out of his system, and he'll storm off and go and cool down somewhere.

For a moment he pauses, and hope rises high in my chest. But suddenly he drops to the floor beside me and he wraps his massive hands around my throat and begins to squeeze. I gasp for air, my attempts to breathe thwarted by his constricting hands. I try to pry my hands away, but his grip is firm. There's no way I can rip his hands free, and my own grip is only causing him to clamp down further. I drop my grasp, leaving only his massive palms to crush my throat.

My vision and my hearing become even fuzzier. Is this how it ends? I stay as still as possible, pleading with myself to stay conscious for as long as I can. If these are my last moments, I want to make them last as long as possible, just in case there's a chance to escape somehow. Even though that seems pretty unlikely right now.

He suddenly loosens his grip. Every cell in my body wants to take a hungry gulp of air, but that would give me away. So instead, I take the tiniest breath I can, just enough to start clearing a little of the fuzziness from my peripheral vision. The very corners of the darkness that is overtaking my being start to recede, but only barely. I feel him lean his face down next to me, and he places his ear by my nose and mouth. I keep myself as still as possible and hold my breath, this time voluntarily. When he doesn't hear me breathing, he touches his fingers to my neck to check my pulse.

"Oh my god, I'm sorry," he whispers. "I'm so sorry."

Oh my god. He thinks I'm dead. He thinks he's killed me, and now he's suddenly full of apologies. But I can't help but wonder what he's sorry for. For hurting me like this? Or because he thinks he's killed me and he's going to spend the rest of his life in prison. For someone so terrified of prison, he's certainly ballsy, treating his domestic partner this way. It's not the first time, and it only seems to be getting worse. It's taking less and less to trigger him, and the consequences are becoming more serious each time.

Without warning, he scoops me up off the floor. I resist the urge to cry out in pain as my tailbone twinges. It's agony, and I'm not sure if it's cracked or just bruised, but either way, I know it's going to be painful for a while as it heals. If this isn't just a quick reprieve before he goes back to trying to strangle the life out of me. Keeping my eyes clamped shut, I'm not for certain but it feels like he's carrying me toward the bed. I silently beg that he'll just place me on the mattress and leave me alone. Eyes still closed, I hold myself still. I don't want any slight movements to rock the boat. There's still a chance he could be done and that he might let me sleep now.

Suddenly, there's a loud thud and I hear running footsteps ascending the stairs. I open my eyes, squinting at the bright light as a familiar figure bursts in with his gun aimed at my abuser. He's followed by two other officers who also have their firearms drawn.

"Let her go, Clark." The gravely voice is stern but calm. And he knows my boyfriend's name because these men are far from strangers.

Hatred swirls in my boyfriend's eyes as he glances from the officers and back to me, but as he assesses the situation, he clearly realizes he has no choice but to release his grip on me and place me on the ground.

The moment he does, I yank myself away and run behind the officers. My entire body hurts like hell, but their presence seems to have given me a surge of adrenalin.

"Go! There's an ambulance on its way," one of them says, gesturing toward the door. "Someone will help you."

I don't look back, and as I stumble out into the upper story hallway, a fourth officer meets me and puts my arm around their shoulder for support so I don't have to put weight on my twisted ankle.

I hobble down the stairs with their assistance, and by the time we make it through the living room I hear sirens approaching. The officer has me take a seat on the couch and brings me a glass of water, and the ambulance soon pulls up in the driveway. Blue and red lights flash across the living room.

The officer's radio crackles. "We have him secured. Let us know when all is clear." It's Donovan, the first officer to enter the room with his gun pointed at my boyfriend, Clark. His voice sounds different on the radio, but I'd recognize it anywhere. You get used to a guy's voice when you've dated him for five years, even if he's now your ex.

He clearly wants to make sure they don't perp walk Clark past me while I'm sitting here like this. Trying to keep us separated, to keep me safe and give me some dignity.

The paramedics enter through the front door. Noticing my shivering, one wraps a lightweight silver mylar blanket around my shoulders, and they assist me out the door and into the waiting ambulance. Through the back doors of the vehicle, I see Clark being led out of our apartment, handcuffs firmly securing his wrists behind his back. He shrugs aggressively as he tries to shake off the grip of the cop who escorts him to the waiting police vehicle, its lights flashing eerie red and blue. Aggressive and fighting to the end, just like always.

My tailbone throbs as the EMTs begin to check my vital signs. One dabs at the blood that's formed a crust across my chin and cheek. I see the police vehicle pull away just before we do. Clark glares out the rear window at the back door of the ambulance, nostrils flared. A brief thought races through my head. I hope he acts this way in his cell and someone roughs him up. A cop or another prisoner. Because he certainly deserves it. At the very least, the thought of him spending at least one night in a cold, uncomfortable cell brings me a hint of comfort. Even a flicker of amusement. He hates not being in control.

Still, now's not the time for schadenfreude. I have a lot of reflecting to do. I thought I could get him to change, that I might be the one who could get him to stop behaving in this way. But somehow, he's only getting more emboldened, his punishments becoming more severe.

Tonight was a very close call, and if it wasn't for Donovan, it might have been my last.

The week before

My hands tremble as I lift the cigarette to my mouth and take a drag.

I don't even like the taste of cigarettes, or the slightly out-of-it way they make me feel. Some people call it a buzz. To me, it's a mild numbness that doesn't match the much more efficient buzz of alcohol.

But I've become scared to go home, and now I've found cigarettes to be an excuse to take a time out when Clark's mood starts to go dark. It seems much more palatable to say I'm going outside for a smoke than that I'm off to take a few shots of tequila just so I can get through the evening. I know cigarettes aren't healthy, but neither is my life right now.

I'm not quite sure how we got here in this relationship. It started off with him being so kind and caring. He'd take me out for nice dinners and buy me unexpected gifts. Back then I felt pampered and spoiled, like some kind of modern-day princess. He made me feel special and made me feel seen in a way that nobody else ever had. He was doing pretty well in his career, and was well-liked by a wide circle of friends and close with his large family.

But as the months went on, I started to notice a pattern. His outward displays of affection tended to be in front of other people, and he'd act quite different when we were home alone, just the two of us. And over time, the kind gestures began to fade and were replaced with little jabs. Little comments that to an innocent ear might sound like a friendly in-joke between a bantering couple but to me felt like increasingly larger knives twisting in my gut.

These days, I'm never sure what kind of mood he's going to be in, or what I'm going to be accused of. Sometimes he'll scream that I'm cheating with the Amazon delivery guy or the neighbor's teenage son. Other times he'll complain that I've put on weight even though the scales have only moved downward since I met him. At first it was an intentional attempt to look good for him, and he's made it clear he prefers women to be skinny, but now it's just difficult to have an appetite.

Sometimes he'll be mad because I apparently haven't put my dishes in the dishwasher the right way. Other days it'll be because he thinks

I should be doing more with my life, and that my career should be as far along as his. Once it was because I got a holiday bonus at work that was larger than the one he received. My cooking is too bland but also too flavorful. My clothing is too revealing but also too frumpy. My cleaning isn't up to par with the way his mother keeps a house. My tone of voice is irritating. I'm just wrong. Wrong. Wrong.

It doesn't matter how big or small my alleged inadequacies are, or whether his version of the truth is anywhere near accurate. I've become his target, his outlet for his own inner torment. I am the focus of his hatred, his rage. And I'm beginning to wonder if I'll ever be able to escape.

One day after the attack

"Ho-how did you know what was going on?" I can barely bring myself to meet Donovan's eyes, but I want answers, so I reluctantly drag my gaze to meet his. Sure enough, he's assessing me with a concerned expression, the only one he seems to have on his face when he looks at me these days.

My body is tense, my shoulders squeezed tight and high against my body as if they're trying to become earrings. Various monitors beep at my bedside, my hospital gown scratchy against my bruised skin. My tailbone emits a constant, dull thud that makes it uncomfortable to sit up. I'm atop a donut cushion, propped up with my back against a pile of pillows, but it doesn't seem to be doing much.

My throat feels incredibly scratchy and feels like it's full of razor blades each time I swallow. I guess that's what you can expect when someone tries to squeeze the life out of you. The doctors gave me the all-clear for permanent damage, but they did warn me that any type of strangulation can lead to a stroke down the line. It's like a horrific gift that keeps on giving. Basically saying 'you're fine now but you might not actually be fine.' Great.

"Before we go there, how are you feeling, Ruby?" He sits on a shiny wheeled vinyl stool at my bedside, his tall and lanky frame hunched over with his forearms resting on the bed beside my thigh. His close-cropped brown hair is ruffled as if he didn't get much sleep or a chance to brush it this morning. I notice a blanket and a pillow on the overstuffed armchair in the corner, and get the feeling he slept here overnight, unwilling to leave my side. As far as exes go, he's proved himself to be a pretty loyal one. If only he hadn't been such a jerk when he was my actual boyfriend. And if only it wasn't so difficult to date a cop. We're much better off as exes, that's for sure.

His concerned gaze studies the parts of my body not covered by my scratchy gown, and I notice his chocolate brown eyes linger on the maze of bruises that adorn both of my arms, and the fat lip that threatens to once again split and ooze more blood across my face. Defensively, I lift my hand to cover my mouth but wince as my shoulder twinges. It's the one that hit the wall first when Clark threw me against it.

"Like a sack of shit," I reply, and he smirks at my ladylike description. "Look at me." I gesture at myself and wince at the effort. "I'm a regular labyrinth of bruises."

"Yeah, he sure smacked you up pretty good this time." His eyes narrow. He removes his forearms from my bed and jams them into his pockets. "I'm just relieved we got there when we did. But I want to know about you. What did the doctor say when he came in to speak with you before?"

I try to shrug, but my shoulder twinges again. "He said I'm going to be fine. The bruises are just going to hurt for a while. The lip should settle down in a couple of days, although based on what I saw in the mirror earlier, I really think I should look into facial fillers. I feel like this makes me look like one of those Instagram filters. Isn't it alluring?" I wiggle my bottom lip at him in mock seduction, but stop when it feels like the split is about to open up again. A hint of a smile plays across his face and he shakes his head. One of my main coping mechanisms is humor, especially in dark situations. He knows this about me. "And then there's this..." I say, gesturing at my tailbone. "As hot of a fashion accessory as this donut cushion is, I'm hoping I won't need it for much longer. My tailbone hurts like hell."

"Your coccyx, I believe it's called," he says with a wry smile on his face, and I also smirk because I'm immature.

"That's what she said," I say, and he rolls his eyes in mock frustration. "Those are a bitch when they're injured," he empathizes. "I've done it before. Slipped over while chasing a criminal away from a burglary scene. Tripped over on a slip and slide, would you believe it? It's going to hurt for a while, I'm afraid, based on my own experience."

"Yeah, like four weeks or more, they said. Luckily, it's only a bad bruise, and it's not actually fractured." I couldn't bear dealing with this pain for more than a month. It's driving me nuts already, and it's been less than 24 hours.

"Well, everyone's going to be jealous of your fancy tushy pillow until then," he smirks, reflecting my humor back at me even though his facial expression is tense. He knows I need it right now, even though cracking jokes is the last thing on his mind.

I know I'm probably about to get a lecture, and I'm not in the mood for it. While I'm still processing what happened, I don't need anyone else even hinting that this is my fault. But I'm also captive in a hospital bed and he does care about me. I sigh in resignation. Bring on the barrage of domestic violence statistics and the list of resources available to help me. I've heard it all before. It's just a lot and more difficult than anyone understands. Especially when Clark is so skilled at love bombing me and making it seem like he does genuinely want to reset things. It just seems safer and more simple to stay.

"Anyway, enough about me. I'm in expert hands here." To emphasize my point, I gesture around the immaculate hospital room, with state-of-the-art equipment beeping in the background. I'm not looking forward to seeing the bill when I get out of here, even with fairly decent insurance, but I'll worry about that later. "How did you know something bad was going on? Why did you show up at my apartment like you did? I didn't call for help, and I certainly know Clark didn't. And our apartment is pretty soundproof. I know from experience the neighbors don't have a trigger finger to call 911 at the slightest sound, either."

"I know you pretty well, Ruby." He shrugs, his voice brimming with concern. "And even though you've been distancing yourself from your family and friends for a while now, including me, the times we have interacted, I could tell something was off. The distancing was in itself a telltale sign things weren't okay."

"But what was it about yesterday that was different? I didn't even know he was going to fly off the handle until he did, and it all happened so quickly."

He doesn't reply immediately. I know these pregnant pauses. They mean he's putting off saying what's really on his mind, like a little delay tactic in case I get distracted by another shiny object that will let him off the hook, at least temporarily. I'm not falling for it.

"Well? Don't hold back. What was it about today?"

He sighs. "Because I've been keeping an eye on you, Ruby. I felt in my gut that things were escalating. I tried to call you earlier in the day but you weren't answering, so I drove by and heard screaming from the upstairs window. So I radioed for backup. Your apartment isn't as soundproof as you think. I just think a lot of neighbors prefer to stay out of domestic disputes, and hope that someone else will make the call." His voice lowers. "From experience, they often only call once they think someone is actually being murdered."

I let his words sink in. "So you were following me around? Like a stalker?" I jut my lower lip in a pout. Sure, he saved me, but he doesn't need to be following me around all over the place. "You could have gotten in trouble for that, doing personal jobs while you're on duty."

He presses his lips together in a thin line. "Listen, my gut was telling me things weren't okay, alright? I was in the neighborhood and I just needed to drive by and make sure you were safe. Which clearly you were not."

"Well, thank you," I grumble. I don't like that he felt like I needed to be protected. Even though I obviously did need some help yesterday.

"I'm just glad I did, and that we could get to you in time." He reaches out a hand and gently touches my arm, taking care to find a small spot with no bruises.

I flinch at the sensation of being touched, and he immediately notices and moves his large hand away and rests it on the bed.

For some reason, I feel defensive. I don't need my ex riding in like a knight in shining armor and talking about my current boyfriend, no matter what he did to me. Besides, I must have done something to piss him off. It's not like he would have just started attacking me out of nowhere. "He was starting to back off. I think he was carrying me to the bed when you came racing in. I would have been fine."

"Starting to *back off*?" His voice grows uncharacteristically loud, and he gestures with his hands, drawing curious glances through the long vertical windows in the hospital door from a couple of nurses that are walking past my room. "By carrying your semi-conscious body over to the bed? That's what you describe as backing off? Can you even hear yourself right now? God knows what he would have done if we hadn't come in. You would have been lying there, injured and vulnerable and..." He trails off as he notices a nurse stop and peer into the room, as well as my body shrinking into itself in an attempt to disappear. His voice softens as he reaches his large hand out to cover my own. I can feel myself trembling slightly, and the presence of his hand allows mine to still. "Listen, Ruby. I don't mean to sound like I'm angry with you. Because I'm not angry with you at all. And I didn't mean to raise my voice. Justifying the type of behavior you've endured is completely normal in these situations. But one day, I hope you'll look back and realize how much this guy has gotten into your head. That you've been able to rationalize even the most outrageous, hideous behavior. That he's putting your life and everything you've ever worked for at risk. And that you never deserved to put up with any of it."

I sigh, relieved that he's backing off but also frustrated that he's once again being the sensible one. The voice of reason. He makes things sound so straightforward when they're really not at all. "Look, I know you have my best interests at heart, Donovan. But this all just happened and I need time to process. I can't just turn off a switch and suddenly hate the guy I've spent the past two years of my life in a relationship with. No matter what he did. I need to work through it and try to understand what happened."

"And nobody is asking you to figure it out overnight, even though it can be frustrating as hell at times to see you keep going through this. I know you're not the type of person who can just cut someone off cold. Anyone. Your relationship with your mother is testament to that."

I sigh. "Please, don't layer on my maternal issues. This Clark situation is already enough for me to handle. Anyway, is he still in jail? Do you know when he's getting out?"

"It's the weekend, so he'll be staying in until Monday unless someone bails him out before that." He shoots me a warning look, and I put my hands up in defense and shake my head. I'm not planning on bailing him out this time, even though I have before. "I can arrange for a police escort to help you gather some of your things, but I don't think you should stay there and I don't think you should be there when he gets home."

"But we're both on the lease. I should be able to stay in my own apartment. I don't want to go to a shelter."

"Go stay with a friend, then. You're welcome to crash on my couch. In fact, you can take the bed and I'll take the couch. Just tell me you won't go back there and pretend everything is normal. I'm worried enough about how he might act when he gets out."

"There's no way I'm staying with you. That would just be... awkward. But thank you. I'll call some friends and see who has a space. But I still feel like I should be okay staying in my own place. Maybe the time in jail has given him some time to think about things, and to put them in perspective. I think he'll be calm when he gets out. We can talk this out."

He lowers his head and presses his lips together, and his Adam's apple bobs as he swallows hard. I dread to hear what's coming next. "He tried to strangle you, Ruby. When you're ready, I'll show you some statistics, but this isn't good. Men who begin strangling their partners have an exponentially higher rate of killing them. Of using a gun on them. This is serious. You can't go back to this guy. Next time,

I might not be driving past just at the right time to be able to help. Next time, he might actually kill you. In fact, it's highly likely." His voice is begging, pleading, and it's like he might even be on the verge of tears. It's disarming, because I'm used to his calm police voice that remains unruffled in even the most heated of situations. I think they teach it at the police academy. How to remain calm when everyone else is shrieking and running around in a flap. But this situation seems to have broken through his previously impermeable exterior. Maybe this is what's always going on inside his head, even when he seems calm. Maybe he's not so unflappable after all. "Did you call the domestic violence hotline? The people who work there are supposed to be really helpful. And I think you could benefit from it."

My eyes flit to the little yellow card that the doctor handed me when he came to see me earlier. I don't know how the people there could help me. It's not like I'm in a situation where I really need to go to a shelter or anything like that. And I don't have kids that I need to escape with to safety. It feels like other people need their help much more than I do. They'll just tell me to leave the relationship and quote the same statistics at me. They won't understand my situation. I don't even understand my situation.

"Can you just stop, please?" My voice raises unintentionally, and I lick my lips as my mouth suddenly feels extra parched. Taking a sip of water from the paper cup on the metal bedside table, I sigh heavily before continuing. "Look, this all just happened. I know you care about me and all and you're only trying to help, but I really don't need your lecture. Especially not right now. I'm in a lot of physical pain and I haven't even begun to work through the emotions I'm feeling right now..." I trail off as my lips tremble, my anger transforming into emotional overwhelm. My eyes water and I squeeze them together tightly to keep the salty, warm liquid inside my eyelids. The last thing I need right now is to turn into a whimpering mess. I need to stay strong, and I need to think.

He squeezes my hand with his own, and this time I don't flinch at his touch. It's comforting and protective and just what I need at this moment. "I'm sorry, Ruby… I know you have a lot on your plate. Just please promise me one thing?" His gaze looks deep into mine, his eyebrows pulled together and his head tilted gently to one side.

"What's that?" I mutter, praying he's not going to lecture me more. I just want to curl up under the covers and go to sleep. Possibly forever.

"Promise me that you'll never let anybody treat you this way again. You deserve so much better, Ladybug."

"Never again," I whisper, and I suddenly realize that for the first time, I'm not just saying it to placate someone. This time I really mean it. I'll never let someone hurt me like this again. And I'll work on myself, too, so I never behave in a way that makes them want to. I must have contributed to this situation. People don't just attack other people for no reason, after all. "And stop calling me that name. You know I hate it."

Chapter Two

T he Present

Ruby

I know it's going to be a bad day when I walk into my bedroom and see my boyfriend of two years fucking his coworkers. Plural.

And I'm seeing this because I just returned home early and unexpectedly because the moment I got to work I lost my job.

Yep, that's how my day is going.

The worst part is, I didn't see any of it coming.

Earlier in the day

"Ruby, we're sorry, but things just aren't working out. The economy is tight and we're making some cuts, and I'm afraid your job no longer exists." My boss shrugs with her usual awkwardness as she delivers this surprise news, and the HR lady sitting beside her pre-emptively pushes a box of Kleenex in my direction.

They're sitting across from me in my boss's office. Two middle-aged ladies who may as well be wearing black cloaks, standing beside a shiny guillotine, passing down news of my fate.

My manager's movements are a little jerkier than usual. She fidgets with her hands, clenching and unclenching them on her lap, and she keeps touching her ear. Good, she should be nervous. I don't deserve this treatment from a company that I've worked so hard for. From a manager who has been my self-appointed mentor for the past two years.

In contrast, the HR lady seems indifferent to the situation. Her shoulders remain relaxed and loose, her facial expression neutral, and her tone flat. Her gaze is blank and devoid of emotion. If someone could be described as dripping with apathy, it would be this woman. As if she had the opportunity to leave the conversation for a minute and mindlessly scroll through her phone, she would jump at the chance. I'm sure she has to have conversations like this all the time and at some point you probably have to numb yourself just to get through it. I wonder how she lives with herself, and whether she wakes up screaming. I hope she has night terrors.

For the entire time I've worked for this company, I've managed to work mostly from home via Zoom. So when they asked me to physically come into corporate headquarters, I felt like something was up.

My boyfriend Gerald raised an eyebrow when I originally told him I had been summoned to come in, but then he seemed oddly excited. "You'll have a great time meeting your team in person again. It's so good for connection and networking. You can't underestimate the value of just being physically present among your coworkers." Weird enthusiasm from someone who goes through phases of avoiding his own office like the plague. But nice to have the encouragement, I guess.

I thought maybe Gerald was right, that maybe it was going to be a good opportunity to interact with my team and some of the higher-ups. My imagination even started to come up with all sorts of scenarios, like maybe the reason I was being asked there in person was because I was about to be offered a promotion. I did receive a coveted retention bonus last quarter, after all. One I wasn't allowed to tell anyone else about because they were so rare, and senior management didn't want it to drive a wedge between coworkers. I wonder if their penchant for confidentiality is going to extend to my getting fired. Gossip spreads like wildfire around this place.

Gerald's words of encouragement psyched me up so much I actually pulled together a work-appropriate outfit and make an effort with my hair and makeup that can't be replicated by a Zoom filter. I'm wearing a flowy pale yellow silk button-up shirt tucked into pleated, linen-blend wide-leg trousers in a cream shade. My accessories are a pair of flat ankle-wrap sandals, because I never wear heels, an oversized designer book tote that I received as a holiday gift from Gerald's fancy parents, and a gold pendant with mother-of-pearl detailing. I've even done my hair, using my AirWrap to create soft, honey brown waves, and applied minimalist makeup. It's the most effort I've put into my appearance for work since I started here, my usual garb being a pair of joggers, a hoodie over a tank top, and my hair tied up in a messy topknot. My outfit made me feel like a boss when I woke up this morning, but now I guess I'm just an unemployed bum in a fancy outfit. If I knew this was what I was being summoned in for, I wouldn't have bothered.

Because I haven't spent much time in this space, I hadn't noticed before how cold and impersonal the corporate headquarters building is.

My manager's office walls are painted an icy blue, and carpeted with synthetic, scratchy fabric chosen for its stain-resistant properties. Generic computer equipment and office supplies are neatly positioned over the space. She's put up a family picture here and there, probably in an attempt to give off some hint that she actually possesses a personality beyond being able to quote company policy in a condescending manner. Hardly inviting.

Outside of her office, a sea of office cubicles sit separated by ugly gray dividers, all devoid of any personal touches because they're 'hot desks' that don't belong to anyone for any period. Only the odd soda can or discarded chip packet indicate that anybody else ever works from here, almost everyone else as keen to cling to a fully remote role as me. The occasional sound of a phone rings in the distance, making me wonder who even uses a landline anymore.

Every few minutes, I hear an annoying receptionist whose high-pitched nasal voice echoes around the open plan office every time someone calls. Greg from Accounting is here, because he loves being in the office and likes to perch on the edge of women's desks and try to get a glimpse of their tits. He must be very disappointed at the lack of eye candy in this barren corporate wasteland. And they wonder why I haven't wanted to come in.

The office experience team has tried to make it edgy by providing a fully stocked fridge full of snacks at all times, and we're even allowed beer on Friday afternoons, but it's still not worth it to me. And by the looks of it, I'm not alone in my sentiment. After all, I can just buy my own drinks and have my own happy hour at home. Doesn't even need to be Friday, or afternoon, that way, and I don't have to interact with annoying colleagues while I do it, either! Win-win.

None of my distaste for this shitty corporate existence, however, takes away from the fact I'm losing my job. I need to fight for it. I need my paycheck. "But, but—I've had consistently excellent performance reviews." I look at them both, pleading. "You know I've exceeded all my financial goals each quarter and streamlined processes to make us more effective and efficient. I just don't understand how this decision was made." Despite never wanting to be in the office, my performance does speak for itself. I've been referred to as an up-and-coming employee, and there have even been conversations about me potentially being accepted into the company's prestigious accelerator program, which has skyrocketed many people's careers over the years.

"Yes, we know all that, Ruby," says my boss, or I guess now technically my former boss. "You have been a good worker and received positive employment reviews." Her words are cold and impersonal, like she could be talking about a barista or checkout person or janitor that she sees in the course of her day but doesn't actually see. Not someone who she can name, whose favorite restaurant she knows, whose partner she knows by name. "But unfortunately, we can't justify your role at the moment." Despite her attempt at indifference, she gives herself away by rubbing the back of her neck and clearing her throat repeatedly. She also keeps glancing at the HR lady as if she's her emotional support animal, and as if she wants her to jump in and save her from this awkward conversation.

I also look over at the HR lady, but she doesn't add anything except for a curt nod, maintaining her neutral expression. Super helpful. Her body language remains muted, and I swear she's holding back a yawn. I hope she goes home and drinks herself to death, the miserable cow. How could someone ever become so desensitized to doing a job like this, where she's literally taking away people's livelihood on behalf of senior management?

"Is—is anyone else losing their job?" I quirk an eyebrow at my boss, and she immediately drops her gaze to the floor.

"Nope, just you," she says, her voice low. She bites her lip and her knee bounces a little. I wouldn't be surprised if she suddenly jumped to her feet and raced out the door at this point.

"That seems kind of personal," I say, eyeing them both carefully and crossing my arms over my chest. "It doesn't seem like cutting only my job would help the company off the precipice of financial ruin." My job pays decently by industry standards, but it's still hardly enough to help the company out of any sort of real trouble. I just don't buy their reasoning. There has to be more to this. Maybe I can talk them out of it if they're not fully comfortable with the decision. My boss certainly seems to be struggling with it.

"Well, I can assure you it's not personal. It's just business." My boss mirrors my body language by crossing her arms tightly over her own chest. Her body language is rigid, and she blinks rapidly. It's like she's looking at me but also through me. Like she wants to be polite but also can't bear for her gaze to meet mine in any real way.

My mind flashes back to a meeting several days ago. "Is it because I spoke out at that meeting the other day?" The two women look at each other, and the HR lady gives my manager a subtle nod as if indicating she's going to take this one.

I'd spoken up on behalf of the team at a recent meeting, because the company had been making people feel pressured to spend money up front out-of-pocket for expenses and it just didn't seem right. People had come to me with their concerns, and I'd taken it upon myself to speak up on behalf of the group. The response from senior management had been cold and dismissive and I was shut down quite quickly in a Zoom full of people, and I got the feeling my advocacy had got me a nomination as a squeaky wheel. Now I'm second-guessing whether it was the right decision to speak up, even though it felt like the right thing at the time.

"Well, we'd of course have preferred you wouldn't have," the HR lady says, raising her hands slightly in a gesture probably meant to indicate she's being transparent and honest. "It did cause quite a distraction. But there's no way we would retaliate against you for expressing your opinion. This is merely a business decision. We have a zero tolerance policy toward retaliation as you know, Ruby."

"Are you sure? I mean... I wouldn't want to lose my job for speaking up in defense of my team members. That really does sound like retaliation. Like a hostile work environment, even. Especially when you just said you prefer I wouldn't have said anything. I'd hate to have to get a lawyer involved." I'm hoping my use of employment relations buzzwords will ruffle the HR lady, but instead her eyes glaze over further and she seems to be doing her best not to roll them right in front of me. To be fair, she must get this terminology hurled at her all the time. But it doesn't mean she has to be a bitch about it. I'm losing my job over here. She could at least pretend to care.

My boss starts to say something, but the HR lady raises up a hand in warning to cut her off, and her tone grows stern. "Sorry, Ruby. But we need you to leave immediately. We're not prepared to re-litigate a sound business decision that has already been made and that senior management stands firmly behind. Please gather your things as quietly and quickly as possible, and security will escort you out." She gestures at the frosted glass door, and I notice the bulky frame of a security guard waiting patiently outside to escort me from the building. A far cry from when I was welcomed in with balloons and cupcakes sent to my house on my first day with a signed card, and everyone telling me how excited they were to have me on the team.

I scrunch my face together and close my eyes for a moment, willing myself not to tell them both to go fuck themselves and burn any of the very few bridges that may still be in place after today. I let out a long, low sigh and urge myself to keep my shoulders up even though they want to slump in defeat. "Okay, okay," I say, softly. "I'll go grab my things."

It's been hard to keep my mouth shut at work as things have gotten increasingly dire in terms of how employees are being treated. I wondered if one day it would come back to bite me in the ass, especially after that last meeting. I guess today is the day.

As security leads me down the half-empty hallway to the stupid hot desk area where I've placed my belongings for the day, I want to sink into the ugly grey carpet and disappear. I can tell that the few people who are here are watching me and speculating about what happened. Whispers and low murmurs stop right as I walk by, then start back up again as soon as I've passed. Greg from Accounting unapologetically tries to take one last peek at my tits as I walk past his cubicle. My cheeks burn, and I bow my head to avoid eye contact as I pass through the near-empty office. I don't care if five people or one thousand people see me right now. This is downright humiliating.

I grab my things. All I have are my purse and my laptop bag because everything else is at home in my office which is all set up for a job I no longer have. My bottom lip trembles and tears threaten to spill down my face, but I blink them back and force myself to hold my head up high as I'm escorted the remainder of the way out of the office building and out onto the sidewalk where I'm left alone to hail a rideshare.

On my way home, I think about how I'm going to spend the rest of the day. Clearly, it's not going to go as originally intended. I mean, at least I don't have to produce another shitty report with numbers that don't really mean anything. That was never a fun part of my job. And I don't need to sit in another boring Zoom meeting with people who think they're Very Important People because of their job titles. So there's that.

But there's some urgency here. I still have bills to pay and I haven't exactly been good at saving up for a rainy day. My disposable income has gone to clothes and vacations and overpriced fitness memberships for the most part.

Maybe I should already start looking for another job, or maybe I should give myself a moment to take a breath and process what happened. Maybe I can spend the rest of the day sitting on the couch and binge watch some reality TV before Gerald is done with work. Comfort myself a little. Maybe even have some ice cream and a few hard seltzers. That's a win-win for me and for him. He hates those shows and I get some quiet time to relax and process. Self-care is important.

But if I do that, it'll only be a brief reprieve until Gerald gets home. I'm dreading telling him about my job, or more accurately the fact I don't have one anymore. He's going to be so pissed at me. He's been urging me to stop speaking up so much at work because it 'puts me in the firing line in an already tough economy', he's been saying. Sure, he has a fancy job at his family's tech company and makes a lot more money than me, but he's made it very clear that he's not willing to be my provider. It's his expectation that I pay my own way, even though he treats me here and there and reminds me about it for weeks afterwards.

He'll probably say I've brought this entire situation upon myself. But I'm no shrinking violet, and sometimes I could probably do myself a favor and keep my head down and my mouth zipped. My desire to speak up can be too overwhelming at times. It's always well-intentioned, though.

Forty-five minutes later, I walk into our breezy and contemporary apartment. I fell in love with this place the moment I set eyes on it. It's on a quiet street where we don't get the beeping of horns and traffic noise. Instead, we get wraparound views of the lush mountains in the background. Floor-to-ceiling glass windows provide a ton of natural light which really helps with my seasonal affectedness disorder.

I walk into the kitchen and place my purse and laptop down on the quartz countertops, and admire the modern stainless steel appliances with European-style kitchen cabinetry.

The building is stacked with a ton of amenities that we don't use, but I like knowing they're there. I'm a regular at the state-of-the-art fitness center, but I haven't even tried the private movie theater and luxurious common areas. Despite my love of swimming, I've only been in the sparkling infinity pool a few times. It's funny how sometimes you think you really want something, and then you don't even use it more than a few times when it's right in front of your face and immediately accessible to you.

Entering the living room, I glance around to try to find the remote, and something immediately feels off. I realize that usually the alarm is set and would have started beeping at me by now—I'm terrible at remembering to disarm it when I get home—but I don't hear the familiar, startling sound it makes when I do forget.

I do, however, hear voices coming from upstairs. That's weird. Maybe Gerald is taking a conference call from home today and forgot to tell me. Occasionally he'll work remotely—even though he'd like to do it much more frequently his workplace is insisting on much more in-office time—but it's not a regular thing and he usually mentions it. When he does, I try to do something cute like make him a fancy salad for lunch. I guess maybe it was a last-minute thing.

I stop looking for the remote, and head up the stairs in the direction of the voices, expecting to hear him on speakerphone taking a call from our little home office.

That's weird. The voices are coming from the bedroom. Maybe Gerald's pacing around because he's nervous. He does that sometimes, especially on an important call. If he does it too much, our cat Freckles will start chasing him around and nip at his ankles, making him even more flustered. I grin to myself as I think about how cute it is when he does that. I think lots of things are cute about both Gerald and our joint cat, Freckles.

Gerald and I have been together for about two years. In fact, it's our anniversary next week and I've secretly made a reservation at a nearby restaurant that's really hard to get into. We've both been wanting to go there for a while now, but even though our incomes are decent, it's been hard to justify the price tag without it being a special occasion. Three Michelin stars, ten courses and a matching wine pairing doesn't come cheap, but it sounds delicious and like a memory in the making. And we like to spoil each other with surprise treats here and there. Not that I'm going to be able to afford surprises very soon. God, I'm going to need to find another job and fast.

I guess our relationship has its ups and downs like any other couple's. He can be supportive but also controlling, and he's put his hands on me a few times, but it's never been as bad as when Clark used to do it. Besides, he's always been able to explain it away and make me realize it was at least partially, usually mainly, my fault. 'It takes two to tango,' he likes to say. And 'you're not the easiest person to be with.'

He's right. I don't just let things go. Sometimes I get snippy with him, especially when I feel like he's being inconsiderate. I need to chill out more and try to soften my approach. That would probably go a long way to fixing things.

If I'm honest, sometimes I wonder if the relationship is right for me. Sometimes things just seem off, but I haven't been able to put my finger on it. By all accounts, he checks off all the boxes. And it's not the complete shit show that some of my friends are experiencing. Even though he expects me to be financially independent, he generally more than pays his way, which is a big plus.

I guess in some ways I'd say I've just been coasting along for a while because it's been convenient and there's nothing downright 'wrong' that I can pinpoint that would be anything near relationship-ending. Especially compared with what I've been through previously.

"It could be worse," my mom always told me, and that's the approach I've been taking. To appreciate all the positive things and try to gloss over the little attributes about him that irk me or cause the little hairs on my neck to prick up. Because she's right. I've seen it firsthand. Things can be much, much worse.

I enter the bedroom and immediately realize he's not on a fucking conference call.

Instead, he's groaning in pleasure while he gets his dick sucked by a petite brunette and her blonde friend, the three of them curled into some sort of tantric ball on top of the floral-print duvet I picked out just a few months ago. Jesus fucking christ.

I recognize the brunette as someone I've met a few times at work functions he's dragged me along to. She's his assistant, a pretty young woman with perky tits and lips made for blowjobs. How cliche. I wonder how the blonde fits in, although as I cast my eyes over her she's beginning to look familiar, too. For fuck's sake, she's another coworker. I recognize her from the holiday party as well, with her tiny waist and her prominent thigh gap that I noticed several men drooling at over cocktails and hors d'oeuvres. Not that it really matters what they look like, but this somehow makes it that much worse.

They're both blowing him and moaning like his cock is a magical lollipop, and to be honest it's one of the most mediocre things about him so they're putting on a hell of an act. I'm fairly certain his hefty bank account from his flashy job at his dad's tech company, and their potential path to promotion by way of group BJs, is what really has them gobbling him up like he's a peanut butter-filled pretzel.

He's lying back, arms bent at the elbow, hands behind his head, eyes hooded with pleasure as he gazes down at the two women sucking him off. They're all naked, their bodies writhing against each other rhythmically, the women's mouths making slurping sounds as they take turns devouring my supposedly loyal and faithful boyfriend's pencil dick.

A box of condoms sits on the sleek metal nightstand closest to Gerald. As much as I'd like to think he's thinking of my wellbeing by using protection, I know he's scared shitless of getting anybody pregnant. "I'm way too selfish for children," he'd said when the topic had come up once at dinnertime. "I have too many things I want to accomplish that they would get in the way of. I'd rather make sure that I have a good life."

His expression changes to abject horror as he hears a floorboard creak under my foot.

"Ruby!" He exclaims, his eyes bulging and dazed and his mouth remaining open. He lifts his hands up in defense. "It's not what you think!" A flush of red creeps across his chest and neck.

I snort, my mouth twisting in what's probably the textbook expression of derision. I cross my arms tightly over my chest as I glance at the completely insane and unexpected scene before me. "Oh, then please enlighten me. Because it looks like you're getting your dick sucked by two women who aren't your girlfriend. Two of your coworkers, I believe."

By now, the women have politely removed their voluptuous lips from around my long-term boyfriend's cock. My eyes narrow as I glance from one to the other, and they lower their eyes. Shock and surprise have given way to a desire to make this traitorous man from humiliating me like this.

I really thought he was going to propose to me on our anniversary, but I guess my intuition was more than way off the mark judging by this curious turn of events. Fuck me.

The women fumble for their clothes as Gerald tries to explain himself. "Wait—wait," he calls out in futility, for goodness knows what reason. What was he going to do? Ask me to join in? Fuck this guy. Thankfully, they ignore his pleas and both hurry out of the room, still half-dressed, and I slam the door behind them so hard that it shakes the bedroom walls and causes a couple of knick-knacks to jingle atop the dresser.

"What the fuck is going on, Gerald?" I hiss. "How could you?"

"I—it was a one-time thing, I swear." He puts his hands up defensively again. "A—a temporary lapse in judgement. I must be experiencing a fugue state. You know I would never hurt you or cheat on you. They didn't mean anything to me. I just—." His voice falters and trails off like the pitiful specimen I've just started to realize he really is.

I feel my blood pressure rising, my chest tightening as blood pumps through it as a million miles per hour. My jaw stiffens and I stare at him, unblinking, in the face of his obvious lies. "You just what, Gerald? You're really using your knowledge from Psych 101 to tell me that you cheated on me in a *fugue state*? Unbelievable."

"I thought it was a dream. I think it might be. You're dreaming, too. When we wake up, we can both just forget about this." His words come out in a croak. A lame attempt at a joke, perhaps.

"A *dream*? We can *forget* about this?!" I'm enraged. He must think I'm a complete fucking idiot. "A *dream* is something that you don't want to wake up from because it's so enjoyable. I can *forget* when you don't rinse a plate or don't remember to put the cap back on the toothpaste tube. It is not a *dream* to come home and find you cheating on me with a couple of sluts from your job, and I cannot *forget* that you have completely and utterly betrayed me, you lying loser piece of shit!"

Overcome with a wave of rage, I grab from the stack of pillows and cushions neatly piled on the floor and begin hurling them at him. He curls into the fetal position as fluffy embroidered fabric squares and rectangles pelt his body. I aim for his head. I never did like these pillows. His mother helped him decorate the room before we got together. She said it was 'classy and sophisticated and stylish' to festoon the bed with these unnecessary things. They've pissed me off ever since I've moved in but he's refused to let me get rid of them. I got to change the duvet pattern, but the cushions had to stay. Even though now the apartment is rented by both of us, it's never really felt like mine. Now I'm grateful they're available to be used as projectiles. I just wish they were stuffed with rocks instead of fluff. I really want to hurt this man.

Finally, I run out of ammunition. My heart is pounding in my chest from the exertion, and my arms and legs are shaking. I glance around to see if there's anything else left to throw, but the TV seems like overkill and I don't really want to go to prison. My nostrils flare as I gasp for breath and blood pounds in my ears. My vision is clouded and I feel like I'm about to pass out. All I can focus on is Gerald and his stupid face. He's backed up against the headboard with the covers pulled over his naked body as if to protect him from my pillow onslaught.

"Are you done?" he asks. He glances around as well, as if trying to map out my next move and see what might be chucked at him next. He blinks rapidly, avoiding meeting my gaze, and beads of sweat have appeared on his forehead. Good. He should be scared shitless of me after what I just caught him doing. My mind races as I wonder if this really was the first time.

"Oh, yes, I'm very done," I sneer. "In fact, *we* are most definitely done."

His fear seems to dissipate suddenly, and he adjusts his posture. His back is straight against the wooden headboard and his chest is puffed up. He sticks his jaw out at an angle that makes me want to smack it with a sledgehammer.

"Well, if you weren't so needy, none of this would have happened," he says, his mouth pinching into an ugly shape as he crosses his arms tightly over his own chest.

"Excuse me?" I hear my voice raising involuntarily, blood continuing to pound in my ears at the audacity of this excuse for a man.

"You're needy," he says, his voice dripping with condescension and defensiveness. "Oh, and you're overbearing and clingy. You never give me any space. You could have helped us to avoid all this."

"What are you even talking about?" If there's one thing I wouldn't describe myself as, it's clingy. Friends and family have always described my fierce independence as one of my greatest traits. Although I guess I have a tendency to be a bit more codependent when I get into a serious relationship. Still, his words don't ring true to me. Completely, at least. Maybe he has a bit of a point.

"You're always nagging at me, and telling me what to do," he growls, scowling at me. "Also, you don't talk to me nicely. You used to be such a nice person at first. But this is what you've turned me into." He gestures at me, an unkind smile playing across his face. "This is all because of you. Can't you see?" His voice is growing calmer by the second, his own words seeming to embolden him as he accuses me of being the reason he decided to cheat on me. In our own bed, of all places.

"What the fuck?!" I quirk my eyebrow at him, but I'm starting to feel a little apprehensive. *Don't wobble*, I tell myself. *He knows your insecurities, and he's using them to get to you. Don't forget who you are.*

His words are giving me flashbacks to my last relationship. The one where... where I lost almost all sense of my self-identity. Where I almost died. *I can't go back to that place. I can't. Use the tools. Don't let his words alter your memory.* My counselor's voice is flashing in my head, centering me against his eerily calm onslaught.

"And if you just made more of an effort with yourself," he gestures at me with a disdainful expression. "You know... if you ate healthier, did your hair and makeup a bit nicer, my eyes wouldn't wander."

"Are you fucking joking?"

"I'm under so much pressure, providing for our household. You just... drove me to this. You are the reason I did this, Ruby. So you can't be mad. It's because of you. Look how violent you were just now, throwing these pillows at me." He gestures around at the sea of pillows surrounding him on the bed and the floor. He has a point. I probably shouldn't have done that, but I was just so enraged. I can see it now. He's going to say that I'm the violent one, that I am abusive toward him and drove him to do what he did. But I'm not letting him win this one.

"You realize you aren't the poster child for perfect boyfriends, right? And you remember you've hit me with your fists right, you dumb fuck?"

"That was ages ago, and you made me do it." He juts his jaw out in defiance. "You got me all worked up, and I lashed out. I apologized for it at the time. How much longer do you want me to keep apologizing for? You really need to learn to get over things, you know. You can't just hold every little thing over me that I ever did to you. I'm not a bad person, and you're hardly perfect."

"It was a month ago, asshole. And I wouldn't consider putting your hands on me a *little thing*." I suddenly feel like such an idiot. I'm living through déjà vu and I just couldn't see it back then. He's just packaged differently.

"I wouldn't have laid a finger on you if you hadn't opened your mouth. You just don't know when to shut it." He smirks at me, but then he adjusts his expression to neutral and his voice softens. "Baby, can't we just work this out? You only need to change a few things and we can go back to the good times. It'll be better again. We can do this, I promise. I can forgive you."

For a moment I waver, as if I didn't just walk in and see what I saw. Maybe there is an explanation for it. Maybe we can work through it, see a couples counselor and work past it. I've invested two years, and maybe it's worth seeing if we can get through all this.

Remember your worth. You deserve to be treated with kindness and respect. Recognize the signs when someone is manipulating you, and making you second-guess yourself. My counselor's sage words once again ring in my ears, and I shiver as I realize I was about to be sucked into another man's emotional manipulations. And that for the past two years I might have been dealing with this without even recognizing the signs until they were literally shoved into my face.

I draw myself up to my full height, which is only five-foot-four, but it makes me feel empowered. "You know what? I can't take any more of this. I'm sick of you and all your bullshit. Pack your bags, Gerald. Here, let me get them for you." I feel my face flush. Did I just say the right thing? Have I gone too far? Am I making a rash decision in the heat of the moment?

"You can't be serious," he whines, furrowing his brow and biting his bottom lip that's jutting out ever so slightly. "You created this problem and now you're kicking me out? It's my house, too! We're both on the lease. Where will I go?"

I shrug, not actually giving a shit whether he ends up in a penthouse suite or rolled up in a rug down by the river. "You're a grown man. You figure it out. Although I'm sure your Daddy will help bail you out of your predicament."

"Seriously?" he asks, looking a little hurt. I have no doubt his father would help him out if he asked, but he doesn't like to ask him for things. He finds it embarrassing, apparently, preferring to receive his over-inflated salary and telling everyone how hard he worked for his puffed-up job title. I have no doubt that he works reasonably hard, at least from time to time. But if his father wasn't the CEO of the company, there's no way he would have reached VP as quickly as he has, nor command anything like the kind of salary he constantly reminds me is so much higher than my own. Wow, in hindsight this guy really is quite annoying.

I shrug again. "Did I stutter? Tell me, where is the lie?" I have to hold back a smirk. I've always wanted to say those things in a real conversation, as cliche as they might be.

"Fine," he says, standing up in defeat and pulling on some of his typically boring khaki pants that lay crumpled beside the bed, no doubt discarded in a fit of passion with his slutty coworkers. I'm actually a very sex-positive person, and I only call people slutty when they sleep with people who they know are in serious relationships. "But this is my place too, and I'll be back tomorrow." He shakes his head and lets out a hollow laugh. "I can't believe you're doing this to me. You always put me through so much drama. Chaos follows you wherever you go, Ruby. This is all your fault."

I tighten my arms over my chest to protect myself and stay strong. I'm seriously done with this bullshit and can't bear to hear his futile yapping anymore. "Okay, Gaslight McGee. That's enough. We are through."

"No wonder Clark used to hit you."

The room goes silent. Blood rushes through my head, slamming into my temples. For a moment, I consider whether murdering Gerald would be worth spending the rest of my life in prison, but instead of committing a felony I take a deep breath. He just sealed his fate and I know what I have to do.

I walk into the closet and retrieve two suitcases. I make sure to get him the ones that are the oldest and are falling apart like our relationship clearly just did. His jaw drops as I start yanking hangers of his clothing off the shelf and dropping them haphazardly into the suitcase. Some of his shirts fall off the hangers, but I just grab them off the floor, bunch them up in to little balls and hurl them into the suitcases. I couldn't care less whether he has to re-iron his entire perfectly pressed wardrobe.

When all of his visible clothes are shoved into the cases, I point at them. "Gerald, get the fuck out of here and never come back." If I haven't grabbed everything, I can mail the rest to him later.

He sighs. "But Ruby—seriously, where will I go?"

"Should have figured that out before you did what you did, jackass. Maybe you can go and stay with your mom. I'm sure she'd love that. Maybe take her some of these stupid cushions seeing she loves them so much." I stuff a couple of them inside one of the suitcases before zipping them both shut.

He sighs again, pulling on a plaid shirt. Paired with his khakis, he looks like he just stepped out of a J. Crew catalog, and it's so boring it makes me want to puke right in his face. Unfortunately, despite being a walking mainstream clothing catalog, I hate to admit that he also looks quite cute in his outfit.

Ugh, why do I keep fixating on his cuteness even in moments like this? Like my mind is trying to cling onto any of his positive attributes, and potentially our future as a couple. As if thinking anything positive about him overrides how he's been treating me, and what I just caught him doing red-handed.

Don't falter because he's cute. Of course he's cute. You were attracted to him. It doesn't mean he's the only attractive guy out there. It doesn't mean you won't ever find another attractive man again. One that truly deserves you.

Thank god for this counselor and her magical powers that have drilled her advice into my brain for moments like these.

"I'll send you your bill for the remaining rent," I snarl as he heads out the door, trailing the tattered suitcases behind him. "And I'll submit our notice immediately so we can have nothing further to do with each other as soon as possible."

He glances back at me one last time as he descends he staircase. His expression is sad and pathetic, and in that moment I know I've made absolutely the right decision by standing my ground. Even if he is still a bit cute.

Snap out of this, I tell myself. *You deserve much better.*

I need to let him walk out the door and out of my life for good. As the front door slams, I feel a surge of relief wash over my body and I drop to the floor and begin to sob as the events of today start to sink in.

He's gone. I've gotten him to leave. I can never let him back in, even though I know he'll try out of pride or entitlement or not wanting to start again, or whatever the case may be.

He might not be the worst person I've ever been in a relationship with, but that really shouldn't be the benchmark for selecting my forever person.

Wow, look at me. Maybe I am finally developing standards after all.

Chapter Three

R*uby*

I call my best friend, Natasha, praying that she'll pick up. She gives the best advice, even though she doesn't apply the same cool-headed logic in her own life. And she's a great listener, which is exactly what I need.

I breathe a sigh of relief as she answers on the second ring.

"You broke up with Gerald? Oh my goodness! How are you feeling?" Her voice bears a degree of concern, but unless I'm mistaken, she almost sounds a bit giddy. Then again, she's a whirlwind and can get excited over anything from a 20% off coupon at a kitchen supply store to an extra dramatic episode of reality TV.

"Let's go get shit-faced, and you can tell me all about what actually happened," she says, giving me the address of her latest favorite venue. "And then we can figure out what happens next."

I see Natasha standing near the entrance as soon as I get to the address, and she waves me over. While there's a long line of people waiting to get in, we're ushered to a side door where we bypass the queue and form part of a much shorter queue.

By the time we get into the club, it's already packed. Loud music blares in surround sound, and the bass thumps so loudly that the floor trembles.

As we push through the crowd toward the bar, we have to navigate a tangle of bodies swaying to the music. At this hour, some people are more coordinated than others. There's a lot of stumbling and people grabbing onto others.

Given the whole point is to tell her what happened, I would have preferred a quieter venue, but Natasha insisted on this place. She must have a crush on one of the bartenders here or something. Despite being in her early thirties, she never did grow out of her boy-crazy phase. We're always basing our food and beverage outings on where her latest crush is working. Sometimes even our hikes and our shopping trips. But it makes her happy, and she's a great friend who I've known forever and it's always been like this, so I'm happy to oblige.

True to form, as we survey the bar for an open seat a cute guy behind the bar notices Natasha approaching and waves us over. "Hey, love. Great to see you!" He nods at me and shakes my hand across the bar, a broad smile on his face showing off cute dimples on each of his cheeks, and crows feet crinkling at the corners of his eyes in a way that suggests he smiles and laughs a lot. "And you must be Natasha's friend. I'm Danny. Nice to meet you. I kept these seats for you." He gestures at two seats at the far edge of the bar and removes a 'Reserved' sign. It's probably as quiet as we're going to get in a place like this, slightly tucked away from the madness of the dance floor and the DJ who continues to pump bass-heavy music out through the high-tech speaker system.

I smirk at Natasha. "I figured there was a reason you chose this place. He's cute! Seems nice, too!" Whenever one of her crushes shows the potential of being a reasonable human being and not just a total fuckboy, I try hard to encourage her to pursue the opportunity. I hate seeing my friend getting hurt.

She winks and grins and wiggles her eyebrows as we take our seats on the plush barstools. "Might as well kill two birds with one stone," she says. "Although that saying is a bit morbid. I think I'll just call it a win-win."

"You really threw all those stupid cushions at him?" Natasha snorts at me and then takes another sip of her fruity cocktail that's topped with a ridiculous umbrella garnish. I don't know why she likes that sugary shit so much, although they do look cute and colorful on her Instagram. Which is the way I think most people would also describe Natasha.

She has long, wavy brown hair that cascades seductively around her shoulders, and bright green eyes flecked with hazel. Her outfit is a hot pink high-necked minidress so short that it barely conceals her ass-cheeks as if all the fabric was sent to the top of the garment and ran out by the time they got below her waist, paired with ridiculously high matching pink strappy heels. She's accessorized with big, bold drop earrings in brushed gold and a matching gold clutch.

Her outfit is much more daring than my own high-rise flared vegan leather pants and matching crop, but I still feel cute, and I'm also here to discuss dropping my latest love interest, not snag a new one. My hair is swept back in a high ponytail, and I've kept my makeup basic with a slick of black cat-eye eyeliner and lots of mascara, and my favorite red lipstick.

"You know I did. I don't know which I like least, the cushions or Gerald. So it seemed fitting." I match her sip with a slug of my straight-up rye whiskey, and I savor the warm, slightly spicy feeling as it slides down my throat. I have much simpler tastes than Natasha when it comes to my drinks. The boozier and more straightforward, the better. Rye whiskey being the current drink of choice.

"I wish I could have seen the look on his face when you kicked him out," she says, her eyes sparkling with amusement.

I think back to the way his shoulders slumped in defeat as he dragged the tatty suitcases out the door. "It was pitiful. I think it's the first time anyone had ever told him to get out in any situation. But you wouldn't believe his excuses at first. He tried to blame it all on me, as if I'd basically invited them over to do what they were doing, and as if I'd driven him to it!"

She nods knowingly. "I'm surprised you stayed with him so long, to be honest." Her voice lowers, her giddiness apparently on pause for a moment. I can barely hear her against the bumping of the loud music.

"What do you mean?" I arch my eyebrow at her. This is a new development. Natasha never gave me any hint that she didn't think we would make it for the long-term and always seemed to be supportive of our relationship. And she's a pretty blunt person.

It's funny how friends will save up these little snippets of information until *after* you break up with someone. It reminds me of the time I broke up with one guy I'd been seeing for a while, and one of my friends was thrilled because he had apparently reminded her of the Cookie Monster all along. Not that I would have broken up with the guy on that basis, although I'm sure it would have taken up residence in the back of my head until I could only see him demanding more chocolate chips in his baked goods.

But, to be fair, I know it's a protection mechanism, that a lot of friends don't want to see you hurt but they're also scared of putting your friendship at risk by calling out your significant other for anything more than the most serious of things.

"I mean... he didn't seem *awful* or anything." She shrugs. "But at times I could see that he was kind of a jerk to you. You're just so outgoing and bubbly and have this amazing energy about you. And he'd frequently make these little comments that felt like he was taking digs at you, but not in a full-on insulting way. More like it was something that was almost a secret language between the two of you. It was fairly subtle, but enough for me to notice. And it felt like maybe you were settling in some way."

I exhale deeply, her words stinging me a little. But I'm also very aware that what she's saying is true. Someone doesn't need to scream and swear at you in order to be hurtful. Abuse can be far more insidious than that. "Yeah, he checked off all the right boxes on paper, but there was definitely something missing. And after what happened... there's no way I could stay with him."

"Do you think his money had anything to do with it? Why you stayed with him so long?" She quirks her eyebrow at me. "I'm not calling you a gold digger at all, but financial security is obviously important."

I scrunch up my mouth as I digest her question. My initial inclination is to be defensive, but it is something I thought about from time to time through the course of our relationship. "It was nice having someone to partner with to pay the bills. You know, he took care of most of the rent which I never asked him to do. It did let me enroll in school to finish my graduate degree. And he would pay for the most expensive aspects of some nice vacations. I can't complain about those things. But it definitely wasn't the motivating factor in being in that relationship. I guess it just made life a bit easier, and was one thing I didn't have to worry so much about while I was with him."

She nods, clearly deep in thought as she processes what I've shared. "Well, I'm glad you've moved on from that trash pile. You deserve someone who is faithful and loyal and doesn't think he's better than you."

Her eyes narrow and I follow her gaze over to where the cute bartender appears to be flirting with a female customer, his hand brushing against her arm from other the bar. I shoot Natasha a sympathetic look, anticipating what's coming down the line. Her propensity for crushing on guys with jobs that involve an element of flirting for a living, and then complaining about it, is borderline notorious.

"Yeah, I never want to come home and see *that* again." I shudder as I remember walking in on Gerald and his two workmates doing something well outside their job descriptions. My mouth tightens, and as flippant as I'm being about the whole situation I feel like I've been punched in the gut. Hurt, betrayal, sadness. A barrage of emotions hitting me at once, egged on by the whiskey.

"I'm mad at myself for not seeing this coming. For being so willing to trust him in the first place when in hindsight there were signs all along. And I'm also mad at letting myself coast along with him for two years. I could have been finding my dream guy instead of just going through the motions."

She shrugs and reaches over to squeeze my arm, her hot-pink manicured nails digging into me in a way that should hurt but is somehow comforting coming from her. "We've all done it to some extent, Rubes. Sometimes it's easier to see in the rear-view mirror." Without intending to, her eyes flit over to the bartender who is now engaged in a deep conversation with another female patron.

"Well, I'd like to throw the vehicle into reverse and run him over repeatedly," I deadpan, in an attempt to distract her and also make myself feel better. I don't actually want to kill Gerald, even though some might say he deserves it. I'm not sure if I believe in karma, but I'm willing to let nature take its course.

"Oh, I'd happily join you," she grins, unlocking her gaze from the scene playing out with her bartender crush, and turning her entire focus back to me once again. "I'll be your partner in crime any day, Ruby."

We both laugh and then take a moment to enjoy the music and people-watching around us.

"So what do you have planned next? In the post-Gerald, post-shitty job era?"

I press my lips together and shrug. "I guess I'll just be open-minded. See what the universe has in store for me. I'm going to try to embrace every opportunity that comes my way. To say 'yes' instead of being risk-averse and making lists of all the reasons why I shouldn't do something. Because clearly the choices I've been making haven't been serving me. I feel like I just keep repeating the same mistakes over and over. It's time for something different. Something new."

"That sounds like a good plan," she says, nodding. "But just don't be impulsive if there are a bunch of red flags, you know?" She looks at me with concern in her eyes, not realizing the hypocrisy of her advice based on how she operates her own love life. I want to squeeze her sometimes. "You're so talented. You graduated near the top of your class. Your career has been going so well until this last debacle. I've always been in such awe of everything you do, and I'm so proud to have you as my best friend." Her platitudes flow easily with the assistance of yet another fruity cocktail, but I know they're genuine. "I'm sorry things are such a struggle at the moment. And I'm here whenever you need to talk."

"Thank you. I love you." Smiling at her, I realize how grateful I am for her authentic friendship that seems to tolerate all of my random behavior.

"And I love you, too." She smiles back and leans forward to give me a hug.

"Cheers to best friends who get you. Thank you for seeing me." I extend my whiskey glass, not that there's much left in it to cheers with.

"Cheers," she replies, clinking her glass with mine and accidentally sloshing some of her slushy blue drink into my whiskey glass. She's the only person in the world who could get away with contaminating my drink like that without me freaking out. "To seeing each other."

Chapter Four

R *uby*

My head is thumping. I crack one eye open and squint in the sunlight, pain searing through my skull. Thankfully, I'm in my own bedroom. I don't remember how I got here, which is always a bit frightening and has happened far too often, especially when I've gone for a night out with Natasha. It didn't help that her man-crush insisted on sending us away with complimentary shots at the end of the night which we definitely didn't need.

I reach out to my nightstand and grab my phone and scroll through my apps. Ah, looks like I got an Uber when the bar closed. It's been a while since I made it all the way through to closing time before heading home. Must have been a good night.

Memories start coming back to me. I shake my head and laugh as I remember Natasha staking her claim to the hot bartender at the end of the night despite several of his female patrons vying for his attention as closing time approached. Each more eager than the last to take him home, even though he probably does this every night with a different girl. Soon, it's going to be my turn to be there for Natasha, to console her through the inevitable heartache. And I'll be there just the way she's been there for me. Hopefully she at least has some fun in the meantime.

I text her, which is our ritual on mornings after the night before.

ME:Hey girl. Great to see you last night. Thank you for being there for me. I have a cracking headache. Will we ever learn? You get home okay? Whichever home you ended up at, I mean ;)

I put my phone down, not expecting to hear back for a while. Although when I do, I'm sure her texts will be full of all the juicy details. Depending on how the night went, she might even call.

I head to the kitchen and insert an espresso pod into my machine. This thing is my lifeblood, I swear. I inhale deeply as the intoxicating scent of roasted Columbian coffee beans resuscitates me from the night before.

While the coffee pours into my cute little espresso mug that also brings me joy, I pop two slices of bread into the toaster. It was a splurge of a purchase. A hot pink and stainless steel designer toaster. Totally overpriced, but I think of it more like an artwork than a mere kitchen appliance.

While the bread toasts and the coffee brews, I pick up my phone again. This time, to check my email. There are a few advertisements like usual—I really need to unsubscribe from a ton of these places that relentlessly bombard me—and another from an address I don't recognize.

You have been selected for our exclusive Program.

This highly sought-after, prestigious opportunity has the potential to change your life.

Upon graduation, doors will be unlocked that you can only imagine right now. Unlimited opportunities for financial freedom. Networks that only the elite can access. Experiences that money can't buy, and that most people only dream of.

To accept this invitation, please RSVP by return email within 48 hours of receipt.

I smirk to myself. This sounds like one of those scams. Maybe a pyramid scheme where they want to sign me up to sell bright, patterned leggings or maybe a supplement that promises to burn fat at the speed of light. Or maybe they want me to hand over my bank account details and social security number and harvest my organs. I know I said I wanted to change my life, but this wasn't quite what I had in mind.

I check the date on the email just out of curiosity, even though it seems like spam mail. The turnaround timeframe of 48 hours is making my brain spin slightly, creating a sense of urgency that triggers my FOMO even though I have no intention of signing up.

I'm usually pretty responsive, but with everything going on I haven't been keeping up to speed with my inbox. It's a day since this was sent, apparently. Time is ticking down. I snicker at my own ability to get sucked into things like this, especially when other parts of my life are feeling out of control. A moment ago I hadn't even read this email, and now it's all I can think about.

Next thing I'll be putting a multi-thousand dollar down payment on my credit card , wiring it directly to some predatory mega-corporation that targets the vulnerable and cash-poor. I'll be selling overpriced plastic containers or makeup with questionable ingredients, trying to cultivate down-lines. Maybe I'll be weighing up whether I really need two kidneys. Or I'll be booking tickets to a poetry convention where I'm promised to receive an award for my newfound poetry talents. This scam email could take me in so many directions.

I start to smell smoke. *Shit! The toast!* Grey plumes starts to make their way out of the top and side of my designer toaster. An impulse purchase last time I was frustrated with Gerald. I quickly turn the vent fan on high on my microwave, and cancel the toasting cycle so the now golden-brown and slightly blackened slices spring up with so much force they almost fly completely out of the toaster.

I glance back at my phone and the email that's still open on the display. Invited to a prestigious program for the elite? I can't even successfully make toast. Opportunity of my dreams, my ass. I hit the delete button and push the invite out of my mind, instead preferring to focus on buttering my overdone toast and savoring the strong, pleasant taste of my espresso.

Later that day

It's been a few days since I've checked the mailbox, so I head down to the apartment lobby in case it's started to overflow.

When mail builds up, we end up getting reprimanded by building management with snippy letters, and I've already had a couple in the past few months. Now that I'm about to break the lease for this place, I especially don't want to risk antagonizing them any further, especially when they have the ability to charge a discretionary two-month lease break penalty. Of course, Gerald could afford to break the lease with the pocket money he spends on a typical weekend, but he's clearly not going to bend over backward for me in the circumstances.

Rows of sterile-looking metal mailboxes line up, reminiscent of tiny versions of the lockers we had at high school. I wave absently at the concierge who has her head down as usual and doesn't notice my greeting. She's meant to keep track of what's going on in the building, but often she's so absorbed in whatever she's doing on her phone that she barely seems to notice their own surroundings. Oh well, I won't be staying here much longer. There's no way I can pay this rent by myself.

I doubt I'll be able to afford a place with a concierge on my own, but clearly the one we have here isn't doing much to manage the building's security.

I unlock the mailbox, expecting to see a pile of junk mail and maybe a bit or two, but the box also contains a key to one of the parcel lockers below the mailboxes. Finding the right one, I twist the key in the lock. Inside it, there's a large box. Assuming it's something fancy and unnecessary Gerald has bought for himself or one of his slutty workmates, I have the overwhelming urge to throw it in the trash. I get as far as the shiny rectangular receptacle and am about to toss the box in when I notice the ornate calligraphy on the label actually lists my name. Who on earth sent me this? I haven't ordered any packages lately other than cleaning supplies from Amazon, and it's not my birthday for a few months. Even if it was, the only people who typically mail me anything are my two aunts, and they like to send cards with cats wearing sweaters. Definitely not large, heavy boxes with what looks like professional calligraphy on the outside.

The square box itself is elegant and constructed of some type of thick, rigid card stock that I haven't seen before. The finish is a glossy gold, and it's embossed with an unrecognizable elaborate motif and intricate patterns that seem to dance in the light. It feels heavy in my hands, and based on the quality of the materials used in the packaging, I can't help but think it holds something precious inside.

Confused and intrigued, I carry the box past the concierge. She looks up for once and glances at the box. "I saw that come in. It's beautiful. Haven't seen one like that before." Great. She doesn't notice glaring security issues, but she's nosy enough to notice a special-looking package.

"Me either," I reply on my way past, and head back up to my apartment.

I hurry inside and place the box on the kitchen island and grab a pair of scissors from a nearby drawer. I carefully open the box which has been secured by clear tape patterned with intricate swirls.

Inside the box is another box. I lift it carefully from the packaging and place it on the counter in front of me. This box is secured with a small, delicate golden latch that gives it a certain sophistication. As I open it, I'm greeted by a rich, velvety interior in a deep plum color. The plush lining holds several items inside which are wrapped in lush layers of black and gold tissue and also secured with ornate clear stickers bearing the same motif as the external packaging.

I unwrap the first item from its tissue encasing and it's a black candle, encased in a glass jar with a silver lid. The wax is jet black, and it exudes a subtle, intoxicating scent that remind me of the ones in the luxury department store that I like to smell but could never dream of affording. The candle holder itself is adorned with intricate silver patterns which seem to dance and flicker when the light catches them just right. It's absolutely gorgeous. I've never been in love with a candle before, but this might be the one.

Opening the second item, I find a perfume atomizer, which is a small masterpiece of design. Crafted from polished silver, it gleams softly in the kitchen's light. Its design is intricate, with delicate filigree work decorating its surface. I carefully spray the atomizer into the air in front of me, and it emits a mesmerizing fragrance. The scent is a complex blend of exotic spices, floral notes and a hint of something elusive that I can't quite put my finger on.

Finally, I open the last item. Inside the tissue is a jewel pouch that in itself is a work of art, made of rich, deep velvet in a shade of midnight blue. I gently untie the black ribbon that cinches the pouch and lift out a rose gold bracelet monogrammed simply with an 'R'. I can immediately tell the rose gold is real, and it shimmers with a brilliant luster as it catches the light. The bracelet's design is classic and refined, featuring a delicate chain with finely crafted links.

The combination of these three mysterious items is intriguing. Whoever sent these to me appears to know me well, although I can't imagine who would have sent me anything this nice and for no reason at all. Maybe it's a last-ditch effort from Gerald to win me back, but I can't imagine him picking out anything so thoughtful. I love rose gold, which I think he knows, but I definitely hadn't told him about the time I'd spent inhaling the intoxicating scents of luxury fragrance and candles. He would only have laughed at me and made some disparaging comment about how simple women are.

I lift out the last piece of tissue and notice that laying in the center of the box is an envelope. I open it carefully and inside I find an invitation, and it's unlike any I've ever received. It's printed on heavy, cream-colored parchment, and its edges are delicately embossed with gold. The text is penned with elegant calligraphy and hint at a clandestine event with minimal details, bearing only a time and date two days from now, and a location. It's an address in a neighborhood I'm vaguely familiar with although I haven't spent much time there because it's full of mansions and sprawling estates that I've had no reason to visit. Flipping the card over, I see additional text that reads:

In case you didn't think the email was real, or if you haven't read it in time. We want you to know that this Program is the real deal. Consider this your official invitation. We look forward to seeing you at the Program launch. Please read on below for a list of what you will need.

The text goes on to describe a basic list of clothing items, and that the rest of what Program participants need will be provided by the Program team.

Well, holy shit. It seems like the email was real, after all.

And looking down at this random collection of the nicest gifts I've ever received, I can't help but think it would be rude not to attend the launch. If the welcome gifts are this opulent, I can't wait to see what the food and drinks are like. The universe is inviting me to a fancy party, and I'm going to follow through. Program, here I come.

Chapter Five

R*uby*

Later in the day, I text both Natasha and Donovan about the Program and how I'm going to give it a go. Natasha seems enthusiastic and excited for me, like usual. Donovan takes a while to reply, and then asks me to meet him. He's cryptic, but says he has to talk to me about something important. I have a feeling he's making sure I haven't gotten back together with Gerald. But also he's been worried about me. He knows what I went through with Clark and he is concerned I'm repeating the same pattern. So I agree to meet with him to give him peace of mind.

About half an hour later I arrive at our usual spot, the local cafe where we know the coffee is reliably good, and it's noisy enough that nobody will be able to overhear our conversation. I'm not a loud talker, but I can't stand it when people eavesdrop on what I'm saying, and he knows that, which is why he picked it. Sometimes it's nice having someone in your life who knows you so well you can almost run on auto-pilot. At other times, it can be a bit overbearing.

The cafe is busy as usual, a vibrant and bustling hub of activity filled with the sounds, aromas and energy that define a lively coffee house. I inhale the comforting aroma of freshly brewed coffee, mingling with the sweet scent of pastries and the subtle undertone of chai.

Overhead speakers blare music that I grew up with—I believe it's known as 'classic' music now, blending chaotically with conversation, clinking dishes and the low hum of laughter. Everyone from teenagers to senior citizens sit around wooden tables on chairs covered with plush cushions, enjoying their overpriced lattes and matchas. Some are alone and hunched over laptops, but most casually chit-chat with their friends.

The cafe is warm and inviting, with walls painted in earthy tones and large, colorful artwork. The space feels vibrant and creative, with soft, warm lighting hanging from the ceiling and natural light streaming in through the floor-to-ceiling windows at the front of the cafe.

Behind the long counter, baristas move with a sense of purpose, expertly crafting a variety of coffee-based beverages. The espresso machine hisses and sputters next to the sound of milk being frothed and the soft hum of coffee beans being freshly ground. I don't normally eat when I come here, but my stomach has been gurgling and I need carbs to still it, so I pick out a savory scone in addition to my cold brew.

Glancing to my left, I see Donovan is punctual as always and has beaten me to it. He lifts a hand in a mock salute and shakes his head when I point at the menu to see if he wants anything in addition to the pour-over coffee that sits in a to-go cup before him. He's always contemplating his next move, and is more concerned about being able to take his coffee with him than environmental sustainability. It was always a minor point of contention in our relationship.

"Wow, you look a bit rough today," he says as I place my cold brew and scone down on the table across from him, his eyes growing large as his gaze travels over my ruffled appearance.

"Gee, thanks," I reply, taking a seat and taking a giant sip of water from the bottle I brought in with me in my oversized purse. "I even brushed my hair for you."

"Did you? Really? Because…". He smirks, and I narrow my eyes at him in response.

"Fuck you, asshole," I reply. "Anyway, what was so urgent that you needed to meet with me immediately? And why couldn't we just talk over the phone."

He sighs and runs a hand through his hair. His eyes are full of concern as he meets my gaze.

"Listen. You know this… what did you call it? The thing you got an invitation to."

"I don't know its name exactly. Just that it's referred to as The Program."

"Right. 'The Program'." He rolls his eyes but his expression remains serious, and he hunches forward with his eyebrows furrowed. "You do realize that the figurehead of this 'program' is a syndicated crime boss, right?"

"What is this? An episode of *The Sopranos*?" I smirk at him this time. "That sounds nuts. And, anyway, how do you know anything about the Program? Apparently nobody knows about the Program."

He shifts in his chair, but his gaze remains locked with mine. "It's not super public information, Ruby, but I can tell you for sure that it's being actively investigated by people familiar with the dark web. There are murmurs about it around town, and the occasional informant has let something slip. But he basically runs this city and has strong links at a national level, so there's not much anybody can do about it."

"Really? It sounds like you've been reading too many of your spy books or watching action movies all night again or something. This is all so cryptic and sounds make believe. Surely if someone was up to no good, he would be taken down by the authorities."

"Not when it's his program. Plus, he has half of the police force in his pocket, as well as some politicians that are pretty high up. Not to mention the other agencies... he keeps them happy with a limitless supply of his product. They're hardly likely to try to raise any eyebrows. Let's just say he has a lot of blackmail material."

I roll my eyes and snort.

"Seriously, Ruby. Can't you just enroll in a course at the local community college or learn some new crafting thing?"

"Are you fucking serious? I have the opportunity of a lifetime and you're suggesting I go do a crocheting course? Fuck you, Donovan. You're always finding a way to put a damper on anything remotely interesting I want to do."

"Ruby," he says, his expression pleading. "I'm not trying to make your life less fun. I just have access to information that makes some of your plans seem less than ideal. This one in particular."

"Well, you don't have any information that's concrete, and it just sounds like you're trying to crush my dreams. I still think this is too good of an opportunity to pass up. Think of what it could do for my career, for my financial freedom. I told the universe I was going to be open to what it threw my way, and all of a sudden I received the invite. Hearing you may possibly, but not definitely, know something that means a bad person is involved is hardly going to stand in the way of the universe showing me the way to my dreams, Donovan."

He rubs his face with the palm of his hand, pinching his brows and then the bridge of his nose with his thumb and middle finger. It's like he's trying to squeeze what I'm sure he thinks of as 'my nonsense' from his mind. "Ruby, this is serious. I'm just trying to warn you about what you're getting yourself into." He frowns, and his concerned gaze grows more intense. "I'm not going to be around to be your hero when it all gets fucked up. I'm going to have to distance myself from you if that's something you want to get involved in."

This is new. He's never threatened our friendship based on information he's received from work before. "Are you serious? You'll like... estrange me if I decide to go ahead with it?"

"I'm sorry...". He shifts awkwardly in his chair again. "I've just worked way too hard on my career for my future to get messed up because I'm being associated with you and your poor decisions."

I glare at him. "Well, I can't make serious life-altering decisions based on what's best for you. This is nuts. I have to go with my gut. Stop trying to scare me. You're always so cautious and paranoid about absolutely everything. I can't stand it, and you can't stop me." Blood starts pumping in my temples.

"I'm not trying to scare you," he sighs, and he glares right back at me. "*My* gut is telling me—and you—that this is a terrible idea. So I guess in a way I am trying to scare you, but not for fun. Because I've heard stuff that doesn't sit well with me and I don't want you to be in danger."

"Well, your gut also told you that it was a good idea to mix salmon with cheddar cheese last time you cooked for me, so let's really not go there. How about that?"

He smirks, but it's laced with sadness. "Okay, do what you have to do. But you like pineapple on your pizza so look who's talking." He shrugs, and his expression is sad even though he found it in himself to make an attempt at a joke as he's saying goodbye to our friendship. "Good luck out there, Ruby." He squeezes my shoulder in a lame attempt at a friendly hug, and then slips out of the cafe and into the emerging darkness.

Well, this escalated quickly. He's usually serious, but this is a whole other level of intensity. I can't believe he's making such a big deal about some vague rumors about the Program, and that he's ready to forfeit our friendship over it.

He's normally intense, but this reaction to me being offered an opportunity like this seems a little extreme. At first I thought he was bluffing, but he seems dead serious.

Maybe something's going on at his work that he can't share with me and he's over-indexing on the importance of this Program. There's no way me being involved in something like this should have any impact on his career.

I really don't know if I'm ever going to see him again after this.

He's just always been there, but now I guess I'm only going to have myself to count on.

And I'm not quite sure how I feel about that.

Chapter Six

R *uby*

The Next Day

I keep thinking about Donovan's warnings about the Program, but I try to shake it off. Besides, everything he shared was just rumor and speculation.

I call Natasha to get her take, craving her fresh perspective.

"Donovan's information tends to be pretty reliable," she says, her tone thoughtful as she reflects on everything he's shared with us over the years. "But I get what you're saying. He can be such a buzzkill. We can't eat at half the restaurants around town because he's locked up the head chef for something, or knows drugs are trafficked out of the kitchen. He does tend to point out the bad in everything. But maybe that's just what cops do."

I smirk because she's right. Donovan's constantly telling us to stay away from this or that place because he knows about some type of criminal activity that happened there. His cautions have extended to about a dozen restaurants and bars in the city, and even a pole-dancing class that was rumored to have gang affiliations. And if there's one thing Natasha is not okay with, it's being told not to eat at the latest trending restaurants.

It was almost flattering at first, having someone care about me in this way, but it gets suffocating sometimes and makes me feel like a child. Sometimes I go to places he tells me not to *because* he told me not to. Garlic noodles can still be delicious even if weed is being ferried out the back of the kitchen. I don't need him to act like he's my dad or something. Which might sound childish, but that's just proving my point.

"Yeah, but it feels like this is different." I've been giving this a lot of thought, trying to understand why this Program feels so separate from the other times he's raised concerns. "In those situations, he's been personally involved in the cases and has actual information. But for this Program, nobody has actually been able to prove anything, and there are only whispers rather than anything concrete. It's like he wants to believe all the bad rumors are true and have me act based on them."

"Right! That's how I'm thinking about it!" Her voice bubbles with enthusiasm, and I can almost feel her nodding through the phone. "And where's this information coming from? Criminal informants trying to share info in exchange for money or reduced sentences?"

"Yes, that's my understanding. It's probably all made up." My phone tucked between my neck and shoulder, I throw both my hands up in the air even though I know she can't see me. "For god's sake, I don't even know for sure that anyone criminal is even involved in the Program. The informants and everyone else in this city all know that the cops have been gunning for local crime families for years. Of course any juicy tip about their criminal activities is bound to pique a lot of interest."

"Right. He's trusting a bunch of shady dudes and wants you to as well."

"Right. And anyway, Donovan always seems to be overstepping and trying to control my life even though it's really none of his business. Not anymore, at least."

"He does care about you though, Rubes, as annoying as he can be. You know it's coming from a good place."

Her sage words make me feel a bit guilty. "You're right. He's looked out for me when it really wasn't his obligation. He's supported me through some really tough times. Breaking up with Clark was one of the scariest things I've ever done, and Donovan came around and helped me to get all my stuff out before things got even more volatile. I'll never forget him for that, even though he's distancing himself from me now."

"So what are you going to do? Seize the day or play it safe and risk losing Donovan's friendship? You know I'll support you either way."

If I was going to bail, to forfeit my chance at this opportunity, the time would be now. And it's nice to know that Natasha wouldn't judge me if I decided not to go. But I meant what I said. "You know what, Tash? The universe is pointing me this way, and I'm going to go for it. Now isn't the time to be scared or cautious."

"Well, I can't wait to hear all about it." Her voice is like a warm hug through the phone. "Just be safe and call me if you need me."

I end the call and glance once again at the thick card stock invitation with a short list of items it directs me to bring with me. I pull out my small black wheeled suitcase and place it on the floor at the end of the bed and gather the items from the list one by one, placing them carefully inside. It's really just basic toiletries, some underwear and a few simple outfits. They said they'll even provide clothing for the fancier events that are taking place as part of the Program curriculum.

By the time I finish packing I'm feeling even more confident in my choice. I'm actually getting quite excited to find out what it's all about.

There's no way I'm giving up this once in a lifetime opportunity based on someone who won't even drive more than five miles over the speed limit unless he's in an actual car chase.

This is my time. It's an opportunity that will never come around again.

And I can't wait to see what the Program has in store for me.

CHAPTER SEVEN

Donovan

"How are things going with that friend of yours? Is she still thinking of getting involved in that Program you had me look into?" Reeves looks up from his computer when he notices me standing at the door of his office which is tucked away in a floor below ground level at the local police precinct.

His glasses reflect the dim light of his office as he looks up at me from his position on his high-top chair positioned in front of his large desktop monitor. The computer makes a crunching sound as it processes various analytics at the speed of light, occasionally beeping to indicate one of his inputs has generated a positive hit.

I sigh, my eyes tracking Reeves' long, thin fingers as they dance across his keyboard, making a subtle tapping sound. He's one of the fastest typists I've ever seen, while I'm more of a hunter-and-pecker myself. "Yeah, she's gone head and signed up for it despite my warnings. I'm beyond worried about Ruby. She insisted on doing it, because she's so fucking stubborn."

Reeves nods, his mouth pressing together a thin line. "I was afraid you'd say that she'd gone ahead and signed up. As you know, I wasn't able to find any concrete information to suggest it's truly sinister. But we've both heard whispers, murmurs, and they've come from really dark places."

"Yeah. I tried to warn her, but she said I was just paranoid. Then again, she's right. I *am* paranoid. It's part of my job description to assume the worst in everyone that crosses my path. And to be protective of those I care about." I don't say the rest of my thoughts out loud, because I know Reeves is as aware as I am. There's some really fucked up shit that happens in this world. Things that most people don't hear about, that would give them nightmares. People seek out horror films because they think they're so out there, that certain things would never happen. But they're mostly wrong.

Are there really haunted pairs of jeans and baby-eating goblins? Probably not. But are there murderous clowns and psychos that run around in hockey masks chopping people up with chainsaws? Absolutely. It's just not talked about.

"Well, I'm sorry I wasn't able to help you more." Reeves presses his mouth in a thin line, keeping his eyes focused on his computer screen. He seems disappointed in himself, even though he always exceeds my expectations. "I have an alert set up so if anything else turns up that mentions the Program I'll receive a notification immediately."

"You did your best, man. I'm confident that if there was any information, you'd have dug it out."

He closes his eyes for a second, his shoulders rising and falling as he takes a deep breath, visibly relieved I'm not judging his inability to find any information about the Program. "You really care about this Ruby person, don't you? Didn't you used to date a while back?"

"Yeah, it was a long time ago. Feels like it was in another lifetime. But yes, I do really care about Ruby. We might not be together anymore, but she's still very important to me. I'll always care about her and want the best for her. We might not be soulmates destined to spend forever together, but we've developed a close bond that's extended beyond the end of our relationship, and I don't think that will ever change."

Reeves nods, his brow furrowed and a knowing look on his face. It amuses me that this bespectacled analytics genius has somehow become my confidant over the years.

What I haven't mentioned to Reeves is that Ruby has broken my heart twice at this point. Once, when she broke up with me, even though her reasons were valid. My heart healed from that, especially when we got to keep our friendship intact.

But the second time was more recent. When she called me in tears, finally admitting her ex had been physically abusing her for several months. I've never felt more homicidal. But I managed to keep my cool and put my cop hat on and just be there for her, putting her in touch with the best domestic violence resources so she could get the support she needed, and helping her to formulate an escape plan from her asshole then-boyfriend. It was hard to see her continue going back to him over and over again. But I stayed as close as I could, and I'm glad I did. If I didn't drive past her house that day and end up rescuing her, I'm not certain she'd still be here. Things were getting increasingly volatile between her and Clark, and I've seen enough in my line of work to know how these things end up.

Ruby's latest relationship was a bit of a joke. Well, the guy was anyway. Gerald. I could see the breakup coming a mile away. He's a weak-sauce rich boy who works for his daddy and he looked down on her during their entire time together. It was never going to last.

I was just glad he wasn't the type that could really hurt her physically, although there were some minor parallels with Clark. It hurts seeing someone you care about repeat the same patterns, and know that you can't force your advice on them because it will only push them away. It's my role to be her protector, not to isolate her.

But in this situation, I can't risk my career. Ruby has pushed things too far this time. She had a choice to join this mysterious Program, and against my advice and warnings she did. I can't be associated with the people I believe she might be entangling herself with. They're some of the worst, most connected criminals out there, if the whispers are true. Not even I can save her from this.

Besides, the case I'm working on has me very distracted. It's been all-consuming. I dream about it, have nightmares about it. When I'm at the gym, I'm thinking about it. Usually Ruby takes up a giant chunk of my brain, and she still occupies some of it now, but we're after a truly evil piece of shit who is inflicting pain and death on a lot of people in this city.

And I'm starting to think I know who might be our prime suspect.

It's not good.

For me or for Ruby.

Chapter Eight

R *uby*

My ride share car pulls up at outside a large mansion. I'd say I wasn't expecting it, but I'm an obsessive planner when it comes to traveling, even across town, so I'd looked it up on google street view and had an idea of what to expect. It quells my anxiety to have mapped out travel routes in advance, understanding the options and making sure I have enough time to arrive at most places slightly early in case there's an unexpected delay. Today was no exception.

Surrounded by an ornate iron fence and manicured hedges, the property looks like it's from a TV drama that contrasts between the life of aristocrats and the people employed to serve them.

There's a large circular driveway leading up to the manor, but I opted to have the ride share car drop me off at the outermost entrance of the property so I can walk up and soak it all in.

The manicured lawn outside is expansive, and I inhale the pleasant scent of freshly mowed grass that takes me back to my childhood when I'd sit outside while my stepfather mowed the lawn.

Off to one side, I notice a large rectangular swimming pool with an inviting hot tub bubbling away next to it.

A bit further along, there is an ornate gazebo, and to the rear of that what appears to be a tennis court.

There's a garage on the other side of the house, which by the looks of it could fit at least six to eight cars.

The building itself is three stories, and each of the upper floors features multiple balconies overlooking the expansive grounds.

The house is lined with colorful gardens full of flowers and interesting-looking plants, and there are a few water features trickling away here and there. Whoever looks after this place seems to be maintaining it well. It looks like something out of the movies.

Following the instructions on the embossed invitation, I approach the intercom. But before I push any buttons, I hear crackling before a voice echoes through the speaker and says 'Entry granted. The gate will open momentarily.'

The heavy gates open smoothly by themselves, welcoming me in. I can't help but feel like I'm being watched. Glancing around, I don't immediately see any cameras. But I shiver a little at the thought of being watched by an unknown entity, although at least I know the building is well-secured.

A grand, solid wooden door with an ornate brass knocker in the center stands before me. I go to ring the doorbell, but before I get the chance the large wooden door swings open before me and I'm greeted by a tall, beady-eyed man in a crisp grey suit and white, collared shirt.

"You must be Ms. Ruby Hart," he says.

"Yes, that's me. Hello!" He looks alarmed as I extend my hand to shake his, and he backs away as if shaking my hand in return would kick off a deathly allergy. Maybe he's a germaphobe or something.

"Welcome, Ms. Ruby! We're delighted to have you. Now please let me take your coat." His accent is prim and proper British, which is rare around these parts given we're not in England. I wonder how he found his way here, or if whoever owns this home imported him of the purpose of living out their TV butler dreams.

After taking my coat, he leads me into a spacious entryway with high ceilings decorated with crown molding. There's a huge stairway leading up to the second floor, flanked by carved wooden banisters that curl at the bottom. They look like they'd be fun to slide down.

The floors appear to be hardwood, and I'm conscious of the sound of my shoes click-clacking across them.

The walls are patterned with textured wallpaper, and the many high windows are adorned with heavy, luxe-looking curtains. A few pieces of upholstered wooden furniture sit atop thick area rugs. The entire room gives off the masculine scents of leather and wood as well as furniture polish and floor wax. I bet this place is a bitch to keep clean.

"Ms. Ruby. I'm escorting you to the waiting room. We're asking that Program participants do not get involved in conversations with each other just yet. Not until after the official kickoff announcement. Are you clear?" His voice is calm and professional, but I detect a slight warning tone.

Weird. But whatever. It's not like I want to make small talk with strangers, anyway.

I notice a couple of other people being escorted in the same direction, and we're escorted into a room where a handful of other people are already waiting. There's just enough room for us to stand and assess our surroundings. The walls are lined with floor-to-ceiling bookshelves, the contents of which appear to include a variety of leather-bound collections. The decor is masculine, with lots of angular wood and brown and dark green tones. I can't help but imagine a group of older men sitting around in here smoking cigars, playing poker and talking about the economy and politics. It reeks of old money, which isn't something I'm used to. But I've watched enough TV and lost myself in enough books to recognize it when I see it.

Those of us in the room glance at each other, in that awkward way that happens when you're sitting in the waiting room for a job interview with everyone vying for the same position. We give each other little nods and tiny polite smiles now and then while time passes. It's like we want to wish each other good luck, but we secretly don't want each other to succeed because we of course want ourselves to win.

We haven't been told much about this Program, but I'm assuming there's going to be some type of competitive process here. That we can't all receive what was promised to us at the end of this Program. That would be far too good to be true. But the allure of a chance to change lives for the better has clearly drawn in more people than just me.

As minutes go by, I feel comfortable taking more than a cursory glance at what I assume are going to be my fellow Program participants. A few more individuals trickle in, escorted by people wearing the same prim outfit as the man who ushered me in here. I wonder how many other people have been invited and, of those, who actually took the plunge to make it here today.

Looking around the room confirms that I don't recognize any of the approximately two dozen of us that have been squeezed into this room. Not that I expected to. But they all look relatively normal. And surely if something was wrong with the Program none of them would be here.

I feel out of place, even though it doesn't seem like anyone else knows anyone, either. It might be the stuffy atmosphere of the manor, or just being around a group of strangers, but I feel awkward. Taking a deep breath, I try to look relaxed by dropping my shoulders and plastering a neutral expression on my face. I'm sure everyone else must be feeling a similar way, and I have just as much right to be here as they do.

A few faces stand out to me, but in the way that they look like variations of people I already know. I truly think there are only so many versions of faces in the world to go around. There's a girl in the corner who looks a lot like my cousin, Stacey, for instance. She has long, honey brown hair and big green eyes. Her mouth curves up in a very particular way that's almost identical to Stacey's, even though I can almost guarantee they aren't related.

Then there's the frat bro looking guy. He's tall with dark hair in a style that looks like he spent a lot of money at the barber shop. I noticed when I walked in that he reeked like aftershave. In addition to his designer athleisure outfit, he's sporting a fancy pair of sneakers that probably cost a fortune. I feel like I know his type, because I worked for someone like that before. He spent most of his day either working out, talking about working out, or yelling in meetings. Sometimes I was the target of his bro-ey aggression. I'm assuming this guy will have a similar persona.

One guy standing near the center of our group catches my eye. He's attractive, with close-cropped dark brown hair and piercing blue eyes.

I notice him looking at me for a second, with a slight smirk on his face. His sexy eyes twinkle in the dim light of the parlor where we stand.

His confident stance suggests he's the type of guy who is used to women fawning all over him, just because he exists. Of course, he is hot as hell. Based on his looks alone he could have the pick of any woman in this room, and maybe some of the men if that's what he's into.

I see him glance over at the two Barbie doll types standing on the other side of the room, all skinny with their perky tits and perfect skin. They stand closely together, but I get the sense they don't know each other and just gravitated toward each other because they look the same.

I self-consciously straighten the front of my shirt and immediately feel self-conscious about the curves of my own body. Everyone else in the room just seems so... I don't know, perfect.

But that's somehow reassuring, right? A room full of normal, attractive people who are also choosing to be in this Program. Donovan had no clue what he was talking about.

Despite feeling like a fish out of water, I try to make eye contact with a few people just to be polite, but it's pretty awkward given we don't know why we're here and we've been instructed not to make conversation.

Right as I feel like I'm reaching peak awkwardness, trying not to look at any one person for too long, a young woman approaches me. She looks to be in her late twenties, maybe early thirties, and she has straight brown hair and the most intriguing green eyes I've ever seen. They're flecked with gold and they sparkle in the golden light of the parlor's twinkling chandelier.

She smiles at me, revealing a set of straight white teeth that also reflect the overhead light.

"Hey," she whispers, extending her hand. "I'm Whitney. I know we're not meant to talk to each other, but this is just awkward, and I needed to come and say hello."

"I'm Ruby. Nice to meet you, Whitney," I whisper back and reach out my hand to shake hers. "This is a bit weird, right?" I gesture around the room.

She laughs quietly, but in the silence it's still loud enough for a couple of people to glance over in our direction. Her tinkling laugh echoes off the fully-loaded bookshelves. "You can say that again." She pauses for a moment and then asks, "How did you hear about this Program?"

"I received an email," I whisper, thinking back to the curious note. "It was kind of out of the blue. I thought it was a place asking me to be a mystery shopper. I signed up with a few of those companies years ago and get an email from them now and then. But this email looked a bit different and so I opened it, and one thing led to another. You?"

"Yeah, me too. I almost didn't open it. It looked like spam. Same as you said, though. Something about it made me want to read it. I nearly missed the deadline for applying. But then they followed up in the mail with the hard copy invitation and it just seemed... legit. So I figured I'd give it a go."

I grin, remembering how special it felt to open the package. "Yeah, they really won me over with that gold-embossed invitation and the ornate box of gorgeous gifts. I've never seen anything quite like it. In real life, that is."

She laughs. "Me neither. It felt like I was being invited to a royal wedding or something."

I smirk. "I wonder what we're in for here. Do you have any clue what we're meant to do in this Program or how it works?"

Before she can reply, a slender man slips into the room. His navy blue suit is clearly custom-tailored to his lengthy physique, and he wears a red tie and matching pocket square which contrast against a crisp collared shirt. He nods at one of the security men and they move to the side to let him through.

He takes position at the front of the space, and without even needing to clear his throat, his presence leads to a hushed silence. I'm pretty sure everyone else is wondering who he is, too. And we're all dying to find out more about what exactly we're going to be doing here, and what we've gotten ourselves into. It looks like we're finally going to get some answers.

He glances around the room, taking the time to make direct eye contact with each of us. "Good evening, everyone. I am Carlton Winthrop, and I am the leader of the Program Institute. I want to take this opportunity to welcome you all to the Program. You have been carefully selected for this unique and extraordinary opportunity. This group represents the best of the best, from around the country. We've gathered you from far and wide to embark on what we can promise is going to be a life-changing experience for each and every one of you."

A couple of the guys visibly puff up their chests as if they're basking in the compliment, and there are nods and murmurs of affirmation across the room.

"But," he pauses, "getting here is only the start. The fact is that not all of you are going to make it through to the end of this Program. We need to know you're really fit for the task, that you're committed... that you *deserve* the benefits that come from graduating. And we find a certain degree of competition helps us to assess that. And, while we've done our research, it's our belief that some of you do have skeletons. Skeletons that will bring out the worst in you as you compete against your fellow cohort members. We *will* discover these during the course of the Program, so don't try to hide anything. That would be grounds for dismissal from the Program, and the consequences to your lives back home extend well beyond that. Do you understand?"

Interesting. I've never thought of myself as having skeletons, but I guess there are things I've done that I'm not proud of. Nothing criminal. Moreso just lapses in judgement in my personal life.

"I wonder what kind of consequences," I whisper to Whitney.

"Not sure, but it sounds ominous," she whispers back.

The man at the front of the room notices us talking and clears his throat, throwing us a pointed look. "I suggest you pay attention.

Missing any of the instructions is likely to place you at the back of the pack."

A loud, deep voice speaks up from the background. It's the frat bro looking guy with the chiseled jaw and the puffed-up chest.

"How do we know that participating in this Program is worth it? Especially when you've outlined what sound like some pretty intense consequences?"

"That's a fair question. And I can tell you that the successful graduates of our previous cohorts would tell you that the prize at the end is definitely worth it. A life of untold wealth, and of connections that most people can only dream of. After passing this Program, your life... and you as an individual... will be transformed. You will never want for anything, and you'll have emerged on the other end a changed person, the strongest of the strong. Nothing will be able to stop you. You will live a life of your wildest dreams. That is, of course, if you manage to make your way through the entire Program." He pauses and glances around the room again, making eye contact with each one of us. "I will tell you that this Program is not for the faint of heart. But that's why you were nominated, at the end of the day. Someone put their own name behind you. They see you as strong, as gifted, as the cream of the crop. Someone who has a real chance of passing this Program. That's why you're all here. Is your nominator correct in their assessment? Well, we'll let the Program be the judge of that."

"I think I speak on behalf of us all when I ask what does that mean, exactly? How do we know we're not just wasting our time here? How many people are going to make it through, and what's this about consequences?"

They are all reasonable questions, but it's clear from his need to be the first to talk and the way he's holding himself that he's already nominated himself as the leader of our so-called cohort.

"You will receive the information you need, when you need it," snips Carlton. "Not before. You've signed waivers indicating you're prepared to go through anything we might throw your way. And so that means you don't get to ask any further questions."

"But... I thought this was the time to ask questions, given we all just got here and don't know what the hell we're here for."

"Are you questioning our methods already, Zach?" Carlton arrows his eyes, apparently not caring that Zach is basically twice his size. It feels like he's probably encountered this type of person, too, and he's clearly unfazed by it. "Do you want to be the first person kicked out of the program because you can't keep your questions to yourself?"

"No, but we all just want to know what we're getting into here. You're talking about some type of competition, and that not everyone will make it through. We've given up time and made an investment to be here. We deserve answers."

"Did this group appoint you as its spokesperson?" Carlton once again glances around the room, making eye contact with all of us. This time, there's no nodding or murmurs of agreement, just silence. I find myself looking down at the ground awkwardly, and get the feeling everyone else is doing the same. I don't mean to throw the guy under the bus, but we didn't ask him to speak on our behalf, even though his questions were things running through each of our minds. And there's no way I want to be the first person eliminated from the Program, especially for sticking up for a guy who I don't even know and who has supreme douchebag written all over him.

After noticing we've all averted our eyes and nobody is going to come to his defense, Zach scratches the back of his head, and furrows his brow. "No... nevermind. I guess we can wait." Despite his massive size, he looks visibly deflated.

"Excellent. I'm glad we cleared that up," says Carlton. I swear I see a flicker of a smirk pass over his lips, but it disappears just as quickly and he returns to his poised demeanor.

We're led up a spiral staircase to a long hallway with doors on either side leading to bedrooms where we've been assigned roommates. To my relief, I've been paired with Whitney of all people.

"Oh my gosh! I'm so glad they paired me with you and not one of those mean girls," grins Whitney. "This is weird enough without having to put up with that kind of bullshit."

"Oh, I totally feel the same way! Not that I know them yet, but I get that same vibe. You seem like someone I can get along much better with." By that, I mean a no-nonsense, down-to-earth type who was brave enough to come and strike up a conversation with me, which helped to relieve my own discomfort.

"They're just so... cryptic about this Program." She furrows her brow and I can see the cogs turning. "Do you think they're for real? About the prize for graduating, I mean? 'Life-changing' is a little vague, although I'm assuming it involves financial wealth and opening some doors we don't have access to yet."

"I think that's why we're all here, isn't it?" I shrug. "The promise of what could be. I guess we'll find out if they're full of shit or not pretty soon."

"I just hope it isn't some type of scam, and that there is actually a decent 'prize' or whatever you want to call it at the end. I mean, I could be working, earning money for rent and bills." My scalp starts to crawl with anxiety as I think about the potential income I'm forfeiting by being here. "Well, technically I lost my job right before coming into the Program. But I could be using this time to apply for other ones. Someone might have hired me by now."

"Doesn't this sound more exciting than spending your days trawling job sites and interviewing with tired office people, though? This is exciting, and a once in a lifetime experience! And besides, at the very least you got to meet me!" Whitney's eyes flash with excitement and the giddiness in her voice is contagious. I feel my heart rate speed up a little.

"Yeah, I guess you're right. It's definitely not mundane, and at very least it's going to be an interesting experience to look back on." I bite my bottom lip. "I promised myself I'd be open to new adventures and accept what the universe was sending my way. I need to shake this off and get with the Program."

"I see what you did there," Whitney laughs.

A person who laughs at my lame jokes. Excellent.

After quickly unpacking some items and placing them in the large wooden dressers at either side of the room, we head down for dinner as instructed at the kick-off session.

Just like every other aspect of the manor, the dining hall is grand with high, arched ceilings and a large rectangular dining table in the center of the space. Ornate chairs are lined up on either side. Victorian lighting cast a warm and inviting glow across the hall. The table is set as if for a banquet, with perfectly polished silverware and starched napkins folded in perfect symmetry flanking fine white china plates set atop elegant gold chargers. Crystal stemware suggest we might be enjoying some wine with our meal.

Elaborate floral centerpieces have been placed down the center of the table, featuring lush blooms in deep red and vibrant purple.

A full staff of waiters scuttle back and forth with urgency, and off on the far side of the room are the faint sounds of a kitchen, with pots and plates occasionally clanging amidst the hum of communication amongst the kitchen team.

Whatever this program is, they're sure not doing it cheaply, and I feel out of place amidst this level of formality and grandeur. It's definitely not like the dive bars and farm-to-table restaurants I'm used to.

Whitney and I find two empty spaces next to each other and take a seat, because as of now we've become attached at the hip. Unfortunately, Zach enters the room right after us and takes a seat immediately to my left. "Ladies, good evening!" He booms as he takes his seat, his large frame encroaching on my personal space. Of course the loud giant douchebag would pick the spot right beside me. Just my luck.

The attractive guy sits diagonally across from me, and one of the mean girls sits next to him, with the other directly across from him. It looks like they've formed their own little pack, too. I see him glance briefly at me and then look away as if I wasn't worthy of more of his attention. The two girls sitting with him also give a cursory glance before refocusing their attention on Attractive Guy. Almost as if I don't exist.

I try to shrug it off by focusing on what's going on around us, which isn't too hard because there's a lot of activity going on as servers ferry a plethora of dishes to our table. Whitney gives me a funny look. "You okay?"

"Yeah, just wondering why I'm here," I whisper back. "Feeling a bit nervous in this environment."

"You're fine. Don't worry about anyone else. Just relax and enjoy dinner. How amazing is this place?!"

"You're right. I need to chill."

"Someone's feeling out of place, are we?" Zach's voice booms, loud enough for half of the table to hear. A blush creeps up my neck and across my face. "We're all new here, uh—Ruby, was it? No need to feel singled out."

Attractive Guy and his two friends smirk at me, along with a few others from the group.

Zach looks around at everyone and smiles an annoying saccharin smile that I want to punch off his cheesy face. But I'm too busy to fight the urge to crawl into a dark corner and disappear.

The meal is sumptuous, with a variety of fresh seafood and meats served family-style alongside elaborate charcuterie and salads and grilled vegetables accompanied by several mouthwatering sauces and dressings.

Waiters pour glasses of white and red wine from expensive-looking bottles, taking care to wipe the lip of each bottle with starched napkins after every pour.

"Lobster, caviar, prime rib! I've hardly had any of these things, let alone all in one sitting!" Whitney whispers as we savor our meal. She picks up one of her glasses which contains a deep burgundy liquid. "And fine wine, too!"

"Yeah, everything is really delicious." I'm not a picky eater in the first place, but this is seriously some of the best food I've ever tried, each and every item meticulously prepared. "I wonder if they'll give us a to-go box at the end if we ask," I grin, causing Whitney to giggle.

Of course, Zach has no concept of personal space and his bulky arm jostles against mine throughout the meal. At one point, he bumps into my elbow so forcefully while shoveling an enormous chunk of prime rib into his big mouth that the contents of my fork fly partway across the table in the direction of Attractive Guy. The Mean Girls titter at me and he smirks once again.

"This hardly seems like the place for a food fight. Have some decorum," one of the Mean Girls says, her gaze directed at me even though I'm sitting here innocently trying to finish my meal. My dislike meter for them instantly increases.

"Don't worry about those bitches," whispers Whitney, noticing the exchange and immediately having my back. "I have a feeling they're not going to last long here."

"Why do you say that? Don't the mean girls always win?" I murmur back, my mouth full of what might be the best mashed potato and gravy I've ever tasted.

"Not on my watch," she smirks. "And besides, who says *they* are the mean girls? Maybe that's our role in this little Program. I'm not beyond a little well-placed sabotage when the need strikes." She wiggles her eyebrows mischievously.

Maybe she has a point. Maybe this is our time to turn the tables. At the very least, I need to let them stop getting to me so easily.

For dessert, there are elaborate parfaits with fresh fruit, yogurt, ice cream and whipped cream. There are also delicate pastries—custard-filled eclairs iced with chocolate ganache, exquisitely tangy lemon tart topped with passionfruit drizzle, and even tiny little hot fudge sundaes with elegantly scooped vanilla quenelles.

Based on the food, and the sumptuous welcome gifts, I'm already glad I accepted the invitation into the Program and just feeds into its legitimacy. If there was something sinister about this Program, I feel like they wouldn't waste their time treating us so well. I hope every night they feed us like this, although I'm going to have to ramp up my exercise program when I return home.

"They're going to have to roll me out of this bitch," I giggle to Whitney after taking a bite of the most delicious, tangy lemon tart topped with torched meringue. I'm not even typically a dessert person, but this food is seriously to die for.

She's just taken a massive spoonful of parfait and she replies, "Mmhmm," in agreement while nodding with enthusiasm. "Oh my *god*. You have to try this one," she says, handing me a spoon covered in meringue with a passionfruit drizzle. I take the bite and throw my head back in ecstasy. I'm not usually someone to share spoons, even with friends, but Whitney has a way of putting me immediately at ease and not being so uptight.

But, despite my enjoyment of the meal and being in the manor so far, there's also something eerie about the whole situation that has me feeling like we're at some sort of last supper. There's still so much about the Program that's shrouded in secrecy. Carlton's words earlier tonight were a little disturbing, and I'm hoping that it was just intended to ramp up excitement. I try to shrug off the creepy sensation gnawing at my gut, and focus on the rest of my delicious dessert.

After dinner, we all make our way to the pool area out the back where we help ourselves to crystal flutes filled with fizzing champagne. As in real champagne from France, with vibrant golden bubbles that dance down my throat with every sip.

A variety of cocktails and beer has been laid out for us on an elaborate display on the outdoor bar, as well as some little bowls of crunchy snacks. Not that any of us will probably be able to eat anymore after that decadent dinner spread. But the selection of beverages are appealing as we all start settling in to the manor and anticipating what the Program is going to bring.

Zach of course continues true to form with his douchebag repertoire, dive bombing into the deep end of the sapphire pool while yelling "Cannonball!" He causes water to splash all over a few others who have made their way into the pool and were clearly just trying to chill. They glare at him, but he splashes about, oblivious, and tries to get the attention of the Mean Girls by splashing more water in their direction. Great, we're dealing with a real man-child. I wonder how he even got into this Program. Some people have no chill.

Even from the other side of the bar, I can hear the Mean Girls' nasally voices as they chat animatedly to Attractive Guy. He glances over at me at one point and I want to shrink into myself, suddenly very uncomfortable in my own skin.

The food is great, the manor is stuffy but also very nice, but man, some of these people are already starting to grate on my nerves. I'm just grateful to have Whitney.

We make our way over to an outdoor furniture set where a couple of the other program participants are sitting. There's the quiet, shy girl that reminds me of my cousin—it turns out her name is Erika, and a nerdy-looking guy named Eugene, as well as a slightly older lady who introduces herself as Georgina. They haven't said much so far, but they all seem friendly enough based on a few exchanged smiles.

"What do you think this is really all about?" Georgina asks. "Carlton was so... cryptic. Do you think he was for real? Or are we secretly on some game show where the world is watching us?"

"I sure hope not. I can't stand any form of reality TV." Eugene looks down his narrow nose through his round eyeglasses. "This better be as life-changing as they promised."

"It sounds like it's only going to be life-changing for the person who wins, though," says Erika, biting her lower lip.

"Or team. Or however it works." I shrug. "We still don't know shit about what's coming."

"Come on, bro. They just fed us a spectacular meal. Just relax and soak it all in." Zach's voice booms from behind us as he approaches and takes a seat on one of the remaining chairs, inserting himself rudely into our conversation.

He's perched between Erika and Eugene, and man-spreading with abandon so that his bulky legs somehow manage to squish against both of them. They wriggle awkwardly in an attempt to create more personal space, but just like at dinner he appears completely oblivious.

"What do you think the first task is going to be, anyway? What any of them are going to be?" asks Whitney. "Is it going to be like that one game show where you have to eat spiders and goat testicles and shit?"

"I hope it doesn't involve anything to do with heights because I'm really not a fan," Eugene shudders.

"Oh, I hope not either!" squeals Erika, mock cringing in her seat. "I have an aversion to both spiders and goat testicles. And also shit!" Everyone at the table laughs.

Whitney leans over and whispers, "Don't you think they'd make a cute couple? The shy, nerdy ones getting it on? I bet you anything they're going to be together by the end of this."

I smirk as I look over at the couple. "Yeah, you're right. But Eugene won't have a shot if Zach keeps cock-blocking them like he is right now," I say, causing her to crack up as her gaze locks onto the trio. The beefy idiot obliviously interrupting the flirtation between the nerds. They both look irritated at his intrusion but don't ask him to move.

Attractive Guy and the Mean Girls join the conversation, perching at the empty end of the long, L-shaped couch.

Attractive Guy speaks up. "All I know, is that we were told we were chosen for a reason. Because we are the best of the best. So obviously the group running this has good taste. It sounds like there was some sort of rigorous selection process, not like we were self-nominated. Right, guys?" It's the first time I've heard him speak, and I'm almost sorry he opened his mouth. Not that his voice isn't the hottest, deepest thing I've ever heard, so much so that it's giving me a tingly feeling. But based on what he shared, he's clearly driven by status and thinks he's hot shit. Which gives me Gerald vibes. Gross.

"Does anyone know how we were actually selected? Do you have any idea, uh—?" I can't help but speak up, also realizing I don't actually know his name. It's not like I could or would refer to him as Attractive Guy to his face. It seems like his head can already barely fit in the door.

He turns to face me, and I feel like he's looking down at me, which he technically is because he's at least a foot taller than my five-foot-four frame. "Ryan. My name is Ryan," he says. "I don't know the specifics, although I'm sure we'll find out. But they made it clear we were here because of the unique qualities we all bring to the table."

I want to throat punch him as he turns to glance at one of the Mean Girls, making no effort to try to hide he's taking a peek at her cleavage.

"Gross," whispers Whitney from behind her champagne glass, obviously noticing it as well.

"He's instantly dropped from a 10 to a 3 in my opinion," I whisper back, making her laugh once again.

"You really believe that line, though?" I ask, pressing the matter because his unquestioning acceptance of the Program's platitudes is irking me. "They just tell us how fucking fantastic we are and you're going to believe it hook, line and sinker? What if this is all a prank?

What if we're being punked, and this is a TV show designed to make us look like idiots?"

"Listen, if it was we would have had to sign waivers through a TV network or something. The ones we did sign were all made out to corporations I'm sure none of us have ever heard of." He shrugs. "We would have noticed camera people and production crews all around us, and they would be prompting us with what to say to create the appropriate amount of drama and conflict. Besides, I have connections in the TV and film industry and I would have heard rumors about a show like this." He locks eyes with me. "Listen, as far as I'm concerned, this is the real deal. We were chosen because of our unique qualities, and there's really a substantial life-changing prize waiting for us at the end of the Program."

"Okay," I smirk, resisting the urge to roll my eyes. "At least one of us believes it. I still have my doubts."

"I wouldn't say that too loudly," whispers Erika. "You know what they said... talking negatively about the Program is grounds to get kicked out of it. And the consequences." She shivers visibly, and it makes the little hairs on the back of my own neck stand up even though I think whoever's running this Program is likely full of shit.

"Okay, I'll stop with the cynical talk, but only because I don't want to ruin this experience for the rest of you." I attempt a weak smile.

I just hope whatever's waiting for us around the corner is worth it.

CHAPTER NINE

R *uby*

"Good morning, everyone," says Carlton, sharing a thin-lipped smile around the room and exposing his chiclet-like teeth. "Yesterday, you all had a chance to settle into the manor and relax and get to know your fellow cohort members a bit. I do hope everybody enjoyed yesterday's evening meal." Memories of dinner the day before lead to nods and affirmative murmurs across the room. "Now, we're ready to get started with the more serious side of things. This morning, we are gathered here to officially kick off with the first challenge in the program. We call them challenges rather than tasks or assignments because they are, in fact, meant to be challenging." He pauses and lowers his voice, causing most of us to lean in to try to take in every word. "Now, I recommend that you listen very carefully to the instructions, because I won't be repeating them. And if you don't follow the instructions to the letter, there will be consequences that I can promise you that you will not enjoy."

Damn, this guy is strict right off the bat. His words bring out goosebumps on my arms even though his warnings offer no specifics.

I wonder how many times he's done this. His script sounds polished, like maybe he's said these exact words many times before. I look around the room for signs of any previous cohorts—maybe some class photos, for example, but there's nothing to suggest that this Program has taken place previously, and Carlton and the security guards are clearly holding information about the program really close to their chests.

"The challenges in this Program are going to become increasingly more difficult and transformative as it goes on. So consider this to be the most simple and straightforward of our tests. First, we will start with a question to give us greater insight into ourselves and each other," he says. "I'm going to pose it to the room, so we can see where each of us stands."

"This doesn't sound too bad," I whisper to Whitney, and she nods.

"I hope that's all we have to do for this entire time, answer questions honestly," she whispers back. "That sounds like an easy way to make some cash. I'm an open book."

"The question is, if you had a choice between being guaranteed a million-dollar salary each year, or taking a hundred and twenty thousand dollar salary each year, what would you pick?"

Once again, Zach is the first to speak up. "That's a ridiculously easy question," his voice booms, and he rolls his eyes. "Of course anyone would take the million dollars."

"Are you sure?" asks Carlton. "You may need more information in order to formulate your actual answer, Zachary. Perhaps don't be so quick to jump in next time." His tone is stern, and Zach looks at the ground like a toddler who's just been admonished for stealing a cookie. "What if the stipulation was that in order to take the million dollars, you had to cut off all communication with your family or your friends? That you could never speak with your loved ones again. You could never help them financially."

"I couldn't do that," says Whitney without hesitation. "I'm way too close with my family. I couldn't live with myself without them.

And they've given me so much. I feel a responsibility to give back to them." A couple of other people nod.

"Well, I disagree. I still stand by the million dollars," says Zach, his brow furrowed at Whitney as if he thinks she's an idiot.

"Aren't you awfully close with your brother, Zachary?" asks Carlton. "Some might even call it codependent. Haven't you hired him at your last three companies? He's not going to be able to work for you anymore."

Zach furrows his brow further and flares his nostrils. "He's a grown ass man. He can look after himself. Just because I helped him out a few times doesn't mean he can expect it forever."

"He won't be there to have your back anymore. And what about your dear old mother? Haven't you been sending her financial support for the past three years? That would no longer be possible. It sounds like her medication is something she might not be able to afford anymore. And she's on your books for insurance purposes isn't she, Zachary?"

"I, uh—." His voice trails off and he looks to the floor as if second-guessing himself. But just as quickly he puffs himself back up and his nostrils flare. "You know what? I stand by my decision," says Zach, raising his hands defensively and his voice getting deeper as if to reinforce his firm stance. "And please don't call me Zachary. Only my mother calls me that, and only when I'm in trouble."

I resist the urge to roll my eyes, but then I make eye contact with Whitney who's having a similar reaction to me and we share a secret smirk that hopefully Zach won't notice. Whatever this Program is, I don't want to piss anybody off on the first day and risk getting kicked out after what I've been through to get here.

"Oh, do go on," says Carlton, his voice dripping with condescension. "Tell us more about your decision, *Zach*."

Zach clears his throat, probably so he can fill even more of the room with his booming, aggressive voice. "Listen, it's pretty straightforward. I can't be responsible for my parents for the rest of my life. They made their bed to some extent and now they need to lay in it. Besides, my mother is irresponsible as shit when I try to help her out financially. I've done it a few times on top of the insurance stuff, and she's wasted it each time. She needs to learn a lesson."

"Wow, that's cold," says a tall, gangly guy from the back of the room, resulting in a few nods. Dennis, I think his name is. He hasn't said much this entire time and seems to prefer to hang out on his own away from the rest of the group, but from his body language I can tell that Zach has been getting on his nerves.

"So, thinking about your own personal situations, how many of you would take option A, one million dollars? Let's see a show of hands." Carlton glances around the room to see if there are any takers.

Zach's hand shoots up immediately, of course, and then a couple of other people raise theirs as well. Nobody looks particularly comfortable about the decision, everyone with their hand up, except Zach, fidgeting awkwardly.

I wonder about their personal circumstances, and whether they have family to support or anyone else they'd truly miss if they took this option. Or if they're just a selfish sack of shit like Zach appears to be, willing to throw away anyone who he was ever connected to, to torch any pre-existing relationships in favor of money.

My own family pretty much sucks, but I have several close friends and I could never imagine just excising them from my life so I could be financially secure. I'd rather sleep on the streets and get to talk to Natasha every day than live in a mansion by myself as a lonely millionaire or billionaire or whatever level of wealth this Program results in.

"Alright, and who would choose the second option? Maintain your family and friends but make a much more modest, but still very livable, salary?" Carlton glances around the room once again.

The rest of us raise our hands, except for Georgina.

"Georgina. You haven't picked either option. That's not acceptable. Why haven't you?"

"This question just seems so hypothetical. Nobody could ever take away our friends and family. I just don't see the point of this."

"This is your first and final warning. I have told the group that one of the rules is not to question the thinking behind the Program. And that sounds a lot like what you're doing. So I suggest you stop and pick an option. And I can assure you that if the Program does want to remove your friends and family from your life, we most certainly will. And that removal will be permanent. That could happen at any time even if you are eliminated from the Program. In fact, it may become one of the consequences. Do I make myself clear?"

Georgina's face pales immediately and she looks at the floor and clears her throat. "Yes, very clear," she says, her voice low. "Sorry. I pick option two."

"Very well," nods Carlton, his tone softening slightly. "Now you have all shown each other your true colors when it comes to how you rate financial wealth over family and friendships. Notice who picked which option. It really could be life or death the further we get into this Program."

"Life or death," whispers Whitney. "That sounds a bit dramatic."

"Yeah," I nod and whisper back. "He must just be trying to scare us."

As the words come out of my mouth, a shiver travels all the way up my spine causing my shoulder blades to retract.

I really hope I'm right.

CHAPTER TEN

R *yan*

This place is not what I expected.

Then again, I'm not sure what I really expected.

This whole Program has been cryptic and mysterious from the beginning.

I was suspicious when I received an email inviting me to join an exclusive, elite program that could change my life. At best, it sounded like a phishing scam that was going to ask me for my credit card details and social security number. At worst, I figured one of my exes was trolling me, and wanted me to meet up in a dark alley where they'd hired someone to cut my dick off or something.

To be fair, if they had I would probably deserve it given the way I've treated most of them. And there's quite the long list.

But then, I got the invite in the mail with some mysterious gifts, and it made everything seem much more legit. Still mysterious, but it turned the Program into something I wanted to find out more about.

The manor we're staying in is old and grand, where I was anticipating something more contemporary and sleek. It's definitely nothing like my apartment, with its simple lines and monochrome accents. And instead of overlooking the ocean, we're in the middle of a densely wooded area. We're out of my comfort zone, you might say, but that doesn't phase me.

They've paired me as roommates with a quiet, gangly guy named Dennis. He's a little younger than most of the people in this group, and mainly sticks to himself. Which is good. I'd hate to have been paired with a chatty Cathy. And thank god I wasn't paired with that douche canoe, Zach.

I'm determined to win the prize at the end of this challenge, whatever that might be. And if anyone can, I know it's me. Some might call me a cocky asshole... okay, a lot of people do. But it's not my fault I've always naturally enjoyed a challenge. That's part of what made this Program thing too intriguing to pass up. The fact I've never heard of it, and there is no trace of it online from what I can see, is also compelling. I don't like not knowing about things, especially when they're meant to be exclusive and elite. The more I looked, the less I found. So now I'm here to find out about it all for myself.

The first challenge was super simple. In fact, I almost laughed when Carlton posed the question. I've done a few ethics courses at business school, so I wasn't surprised that answers were across the board. Some people will do anything for money, and many of them aren't afraid to admit it. They're proud, even. If every challenge is this simple, I'll actually be very disappointed. And I can't imagine the prize for graduating is worth much if that's all we have to do. It would just be far too easy for anything worthwhile to be waiting at the end. Then again, maybe I should be careful what I wish for.

As for the group, well... it's quite the eclectic bunch.

That frat bro guy Zach won't shut the fuck up. It's irritating, the way he swanned in here and assumed we were all going to follow his lead. Who the fuck does he think he is? Clearly he doesn't have any idea who I am, or he wouldn't have been so quick to try to suck all the air out of the room with his idiotic booming voice.

We're both big guys, around the same size, but he's obviously posturing and trying to make himself the alpha here. Gross. I'll put him in his place the moment I get a chance. Although, he almost got himself kicked out of the Program already, so maybe I won't have an opportunity to take him down myself. Pity.

Then there are the two blonde girls. They're both all over me, and truth be told I find it difficult to tell them apart because they look and act and sound so similar. They're both attractive, and they're fawning all over me the way I'm used to most women doing, and we've formed some kind of clique I guess you could call it. But they're not exciting to me. They're just... there. Of course, I'm not against a little flirtation or maybe even something more.

Then there's Ruby. There's something different about her. I've seen her looking at me a couple of times, but not in the same way as the other girls. It's like her gaze sees into me, like she's intrigued by me and trying to figure me out. And she's very pretty, but I get the feeling she doesn't realize it.

Georgina, Eugene and Erika have also formed a tight-knit little group. They seem to be the most introverted ones, not trying to cause any bother and huddling together to speak in hushed tones. No doubt they're also just trying to figure out what's going on here. I think there might be something brewing between Erika and Eugene.

Dennis, the loner, is always off to the side or back of the room, barely saying a word. Again, the ideal roommate from my perspective.

And there are several other participants, but I haven't really spoken with them yet.

But based on my assessment, there's nobody here who could come close to beating me, no matter what the challenges entail.

I'm clearly the best and brightest of them all.

And I'm going to win this thing if it's the last thing I do.

Chapter Eleven

R *uby*

We're once again in the parlor where the Program first kicked off, but now we're seated in rows of neatly arranged chairs upholstered in plush fabric. Carlton stands at the front of the room behind a sleek metal podium that contrasts with the dark, ornate wood in the masculine space.

"Good afternoon, Cohort. I trust you have all reflected on the answers given in the first challenge, and that it has given you insight into your fellow cohort members."

A few of us nod and shoot glances at the people who opted for the million dollars, especially Zach.

"For the next challenge, you will allow us to go through your phone and review all prior communication history, including pictures and browser search history."

I smirk as the atmosphere in the room immediately shifts. And particularly at the guys who shuffle uncomfortably from one foot to the other. A couple of the girls are also blushing at this point.

Whitney makes eye contact with me and she winks and nods her head in their direction.

I mouth back, 'I know!' and she grins.

Thinking about my phone content, I'm relieved that I'm not particularly bothered by this challenge. I mean, I don't like the thought of people going through my phone because it just seems invasive. Things can be taken out of context, and I might have a few dorky selfies in there. But for the most part, I'm pretty consistent with how I treat people around me, and I'm not sending nude pics to people so there's nothing to worry about on that account.

Maybe a few of my Internet searches are a bit cringeworthy, but from the way the atmosphere in the room has changed I get the distinct feeling my interests are on the vanilla end of the spectrum. Plus, I am an avid user of the incognito function and now it looks like it's for a good reason.

"We will have the ability to share anything we like with the rest of the people in this room. Or the world. And we realize this gives us leverage in the future. If you don't make it through to the end of this program, the chances of some of the most compromising data being revealed is fairly high. It's part of the consequences of getting dismissed from the program. So you have the option, right now, as a onetime deal." Carlton pauses for effect, lowering his voice so we have to lean in again to hear his words. "If you want to withdraw from this program immediately, we will give you an out to do so now before the contents of your phone are revealed. No questions asked. Please raise your hand if you would like to take this option."

Two individuals raise their hands, a male and a female. They're a pair I haven't really got to know, but they just looked like regular people. Not like people that I'd imagine would have life-destroying skeletons in their closet, or on their phones. But I guess looks can be deceiving.

I'm fascinated to see what they have on their phones that has them so concerned. Although, on second thought, maybe I don't want to know.

I feel like just withdrawing themselves from the Program so abruptly must mean it's pretty bad. I don't know that a comprehensive library of dick pics would be enough to make you want to pass up this opportunity, even if it's an embarrassing-looking one. It has to be something far worse. Maybe evidence of criminal wrongdoing. Something where the punishment would be worse than what they think the prize might be for making it through this weird program.

"Very well," says Carlton, a small smirk building on his thin-lipped face. "The guards will escort you out. As for the rest of you, your phones will be scraped in the coming days. And we will decide when and what to share and with whom. Is that clear?"

Everybody nods, a few people shifting in their seat. A shiver runs down my spine at the thought of the control the Program leaders have, and how this information might be used. But I'm committed, and I have nothing to hide.

"Oh my gosh! What you do you suppose they did?" squeals Whitney when we're back in the privacy of our own room.

"I know!" I nod, my eyes large. "OMG. Do you think it was blueprints for a bank robbery stored on their phones? Child porn? Dead bodies of the people they ax murdered and buried deep in the forest? Satanic rituals that implicate prominent politicians? I can keep going if you like..." I grin at her.

"Jesus, Ruby. You're warped!" laughs Whitney. "I was thinking more like the largest library of dick pics in the galaxy."

"Are you slut-shaming women for receiving unsolicited dick pics? That's not fair." I screw up my nose but laugh anyway.

"That's fair. Even if they were solicited, who cares? But I just…". She shrugs, and she pauses as her brain tries to figure out the right words. "I just don't know what someone could have on their phone that's so bad they would be afraid to pass up the potential prize at the end of this Program. Well, until you pointed out some of the possibilities, that is," she giggles. "I'll be sure to come to you when I need dark material to feed my soul."

"That's what I'm here for," I laugh. "Any time."

CHAPTER TWELVE

Ruby

It's the following day, and time for the third challenge.

The first two have gone by fairly smoothly, although we're still waiting to see what's going to happen with our phone content.

Screens have been placed in our rooms, presumably to showcase some of the things the Program leaders have found on our phones. I'm not too worried about what they'll show from mine. But I'm not going to lie, I'm kind of excited to see what tea they find on the other Cohort participants.

"What do you think this challenge is going to be about?" Based on the previous two, I'm imagining another ethical dilemma or maybe they want us to do a truth or dare or something relatively benign.

"I don't know, but the instructions are to meet by the pool this time. Maybe a swimming race?" Whitney grins at me.

"Ha! I have a feeling that would be too simple. What are they cooking up for us, I wonder?!"

"I guess we're about to find out. Let's just hope we're ready for it."

"This challenge is intended to test your commitment to the Program," Carlton gestures at our group. "Your tenacity. Your loyalty. But this task is going to be individualized. For fairness, we are going to pick one of your names out of a hat."

One of the guards brings over a large black top hat. He tips it toward us, revealing that it's filled with tightly folded pieces of white paper.

"As you can see, this hat is filled with each of your names. I will retrieve one piece of paper from the hat, and if your name is on it you're going to have a serious choice to make."

Please don't pick me, I think. There are still a fair number of participants, maybe twenty, so the odds are in my favor that I won't be chosen. Not that I know what the challenge is going to be, but Carlton's words were ominous and I just have a feeling it's not going to be good.

"Without further ado, I am pleased to remove a name." Carlton retrieves a piece of paper from the hat and unfolds it. We all crane our necks to try to make out the small, typed print as he holds it up. "Ryan. Ryan Parker. You are the next to participate in the challenge. If you successfully complete it, you will rise up in the lead of our Program rankings. But if you don't, you will automatically be dismissed from the Program, and there will be consequences. Do you understand?"

"Loud and clear," Ryan mock salutes Carlton. "I'm ready when you are." His voice is resonant and as sexy as always, but he shuffles a little in his seat. Maybe Mr. Cocky Pants isn't so confident after all.

"Excellent. Please wheel out the table, Smith."

The burlier of the two guards nods and exits through a side door, and wheels in a cart made from surgical steel. Atop the cart is a large cleaver that twinkles in the dim light of the parlor. Ryan's face pales as he sees the cleaver.

"Now, Ryan," says Carlton, a little smile playing over his face. "To demonstrate your commitment to the Program, you are going to sacrifice a digit. But because we want you to feel empowered by this challenge, we want to give you an element of choice. You may choose whether you want to give up either a finger or a toe."

A couple of audible gasps ring out across the room.

"You've got to be kidding me," he says, his brow furrowing in disbelief. "Is this a prank? Are there cameras around here?" He glances wildly around the ceiling and bookshelves.

"Oh, I can assure you that we don't do pranks here, Ryan," says Carlton, his mouth upturned in open amusement. "Now I suggest you stop asking questions and tell us what you'd prefer to lose. What will it be? Finger or toe?" Carlton lifts up the cleaver, which looks even larger now, the overhead light glancing off it and causing little reflective patches to dance over the bookshelves.

"Let me think for a moment, please," begs Ryan, staring down at his hands and feet. His fingers twitch nervously. "Um, uh, okay—my little finger on my left hand, I guess." He wiggles it. "No, no wait," he adds quickly. He wiggles his fingers again. "Maybe the third finger on my let hand."

"Is that your final selection? Time is ticking, Ryan," says Carlton, smiling at the hot man who suddenly isn't seeming so cocky anymore.

"Um, wait, no. Take my fourth toe on my left foot."

"Are you sure? No takesies-backsies," says Carlton, visibly enjoying watching Ryan get flustered.

"No, wait. Final answer. Third finger on my left hand. Oh god," he whimpers as he looks down at his hand. "Do we really have to do this?"

"Oh, I thought I made that perfectly clear, Ryan. We don't *have* to do anything. It's your choice when it comes down to it. But if you want to demonstrate your commitment to the program, you will need to successfully complete this challenge."

He takes a deep breath. "Oh my god, okay. Yes, I'm ready."

"Very well, to confirm, you have selected the third finger on your left hand."

Ryan nods and clears his throat.

"This is fucking insane," whispers Whitney. "But at least he won't be able to flip us off with his left hand."

I snort, and a couple of people glance in our direction. I don't think Ryan getting his finger chopped off is funny, but it just seems so surreal. Surely they're pranking him and the cleaver isn't actually real or something like that. It sure looks real, though, its shiny blade looking especially sharp.

"Very well. Place your finger of choice down on the table here," Carlton points to the short end of the table nearest him.

Ryan complies, and his hand shakes as he extends his finger onto the shiny steel surface.

Without any fanfare, Carlton lifts his hand that's wielding the cleaver and brings the tool down hard. Gasps echo around the room as Ryan's middle finger is severed clean and bounces onto the table and then rolls onto the floor. Ryan shrieks as he looks at the bloody stump in the middle of his left hand and the severed finger sitting on the floor. His body jerks to the side, his face pales and he slumps to the floor.

"Did he just faint? Or is he dead?" whispers Whitney.

"Pretty sure he just fainted," I whisper back. Oh my god. I can't even imagine how much that must have hurt. I can't believe that just happened!

The other guard slips out the side door and wheels in a wheelchair, and the two men lift Ryan into the seat. One of them picks up his severed finger, while the other wheels him out of the room.

"Where—where are you taking him?" one of the Mean Girls asks in her nasally voice.

"To tend to his wounds, of course," says Carlton. "We're not barbarians around here. We wouldn't want him to get an infection or anything unsavory like that."

"You just—chopped his finger off, though," says Dennis from the back of the room, speaking up for one of the first times since the Program started. "That seems pretty barbaric to me."

"Are you questioning the Program, Dennis?" Carlton asks in a reprimanding tone. "Because I'd be very careful about doing that if I were you."

"No, sorry. Of course not," Dennis says quickly, lowering his head and seeming to shrink into the back wall.

"Does anybody else have any questions or feedback?" Carlton looks around the room as if daring anyone else to speak up.

We all lower our eyes and try to remain silent.

"Excellent, you are finally starting to get it. Now, go have some free time for the rest of the day. Unwind. Relax. Get excited about the next challenge."

A lump forms in the pit of my stomach, the first twinges of heartburn making their way up my chest and into my throat. That could have been me, today. And oh my god, poor Ryan. I can't even imagine how he must be feeling.

And hopefully I won't ever have to.

But I have the overwhelming urge to make sure he's alright.

A few hours later

"Oh my god, Ryan! Are you okay?"

I find him in the annex at the far end of the long hallway, just down from the dining hall. He still looks pale, and he clings to the hand from which his finger was just brutally severed.

He grimaces and blinks hard. "I've been better. But," he says, raising his hand and revealing a tightly wound bandage covering his wound, "as you can see, they've given me proper medical attention. Stitched and bandaged me up, added some ointment so it won't get infected."

"They won't give you your finger back?"

"That's what I can't work out. They took it away, and I swear I saw them putting it in a Zip-Loc bag and into one of the big freezers near the kitchen. But I figure if I don't get it back really soon they'll never be able to reattach it. I guess it might really be gone for good."

My hand flies to my mouth. It feels like I should probably just keep it there at this point. This Program has barely started, and it's already turning out to be perpetually shocking.

"My god, Ryan. I'm so sorry. This is too much," I say, taking care to keep my voice to a barely audible whisper. I don't want them to retaliate by chopping off one of my digits or worse. "Chopping off your finger. It's just... grotesque." I frown. "Not that you are grotesque at all," I add hurriedly, causing him to smirk briefly before returning to his pained expression. "It's just... inhumane and unnecessary. I don't understand it. It's just too much."

"I'll survive," he says.

"It's okay to not be okay, you know," I meet his gaze and almost get lost in his sparkling sapphire eyes. "You don't have to pretend you're always fine. This is a big deal for you, and it will impact you for the rest of your life. You can tell me how you're really feeling, if you want."

He eyes me with suspicion, but then his expression softens. "Thank you. Yeah, that was scary as fuck. That cleaver was no joke. I'm embarrassed I fainted. My whole hand is throbbing. And I'm honestly quite terrified. I'm just glad they tended to my wound so quickly. Ironic, being so brutal and then so efficient with the aftercare."

"I can only imagine. And I hope you feel much better soon. I don't know how to process this and I'm not the one who just had their finger chopped off."

"Well, as you said, the Program has barely started. We're still newbies. So I imagine it's only going to get worse from here on in. But the consequences of dropping out of the Program or, worse yet, being kicked out, seem far greater. So we need to buckle up and hang on for the ride. Even if that means losing a finger." He wiggles his bandaged hand at me with a wry smile.

I gulp. He's right. If this is how we start out, what in hell can we expect to happen next? If there's anything today's events have proven, it's that the people running this Program are batshit crazy. And that nothing, except for Ryan's finger, is off the table.

Chapter Thirteen

*R*yan

I'm starting to second-guess myself. It's not the first time I've ever felt this way, but it's definitely been a while.

And it's not just having had my finger chopped off in front of a room full of near-strangers. Or the fact my hand now feels like red-hot blood is pumping through it, back and forth from the stump that now exists where my middle finger used to be.

I'm used to being self-assured, confident. Of knowing exactly what I want and how to get it. But this Program has me thrown. I'm not in control of my day-to-day, and some of this whole thing is downright weird. I'm out of my element.

There's something about Ruby that's throwing me off. It's like she sees through me. That she knows my confidence is a shell I wrap around myself and lean into. When deep down inside my biggest insecurity is worrying I'm not in fact all that.

That someone might find me out for not being in control.

That's why Ruby scares me so much. It's why it's her face I see when I touch myself at night. And when I fucked one of the blonde copycats the other night—I don't even remember which one it was—it didn't matter to me, all I could picture was Ruby's gorgeous face as well. Her captivating laugh, her smile, her eyes, her lips.

It's also why I'm so fascinated by her.
And why I can't seem to stay away.

CHAPTER FOURTEEN

R *uby*

"If your name is drawn, you will pluck out Dennis' eye and eat it." Carlton's voice is calm and casual, as if it's a benign request. Like he just asked me to change the TV channel or that he would prefer his eggs over easy.

"Excuse me? Did you just say... pluck out Dennis' *eye* and... *eat it*?" I can't help but speak up. I'm trying to remain calm but my voice reflects my incredulity as panic sets in.

Dennis lets out a low whimper from the back corner where he prefers to camp out.

"Yes. Precisely. Good listening," smirks Carlton.

Low murmurs fill the room as people turn to their neighbors in shock.

"Oh my god," I whisper frantically to Whitney. "I've heard of some *Fear Factor* type shit, but eating a *human* eyeball? Of someone alive... who we know?"

"Ladies, do you have something to say to the group?" Carlton's voice booms toward us, and he looks down his nose at us like an irritated librarian who wants us to shut the fuck up in his library.

"No, no. Very sorry," we both say, hurriedly.

"Very well," he resumes. "I will continue with the task. As I was saying...". He proceeds to read out a series of instructions.

Please don't be me. Please don't be me. And as much as I don't want to be the one to eat the eyeball of a live person, I most certainly don't want to be the one who has my eyeball extracted by a fellow member of our Cohort. My vision has always been something I've valued, given a family history of vision difficulties. I even had the benefit of Lasik surgery on one of my eyes a couple of years ago, and I realize how much being able to see well benefits my every day life. I shudder, goosebumps racing all over my body and the little hairs pricking up on the back of my neck. To have an eyeball plucked out so unnecessarily seems so... barbaric and irreversible.

Once again, Carlton requests that one of the security guards brings the hat into the parlor.

"You'll perhaps be relieved to know, Ryan, that your name is no longer in the hat, so you will not be involved in today's task other than as an observer."

Ryan swipes a hand across his forehead in mock relief, but I can tell by the look in his eyes that the emotion is very real. Imagine that. Being relieved that he *only* lost a finger and that nobody is going to eat his eyeball.

Carlton plucks a tightly folded piece of paper from the black top hat and undoes it as we all lean in eagerly to see whose name has been drawn. "Ruby. Ruby Hart. You will eat Dennis' eyeball."

I feel blood draining from my face. I feel frozen, my own eyes bulging as I glance from Carlton and the piece of paper over to Dennis. "This can't be happening," I say softly.

"Well, it is," says Carlton. "So I hope you're hungry. Get the cart, Rocco," he gestures to the side door and the burly security guard disappears inside. He emerges with the same shiny steel table that served as a chopping board for Ryan's severed finger.

Dennis gulps as the security guards both head over to him and each takes him by an arm. He flails his legs about as he's dragged to the table where he's placed on his back and secured by ropes that are attached to each of the table's sturdy legs. He begins to sob, quietly at first and then his wails grow louder.

"Gag him, please," says Carlton. "His wails bore me."

One of the security guards fetches a long, thin piece of black cloth and secures it tightly around Dennis' mouth.

I look on in horror as the other guard brings forward a large, industrial-looking set of tweezers as well as a strange contraption fashioned from thin wire. "What—what is that?" I ask, my voice wavering as I point at the strange tool.

"It's an eye speculum," explains Carlton. "They're designed to retract the eyelid during ophthalmic surgery. Which is just perfect for the type of procedure you're performing today. Place it please, Rocco."

Dennis tries to squeeze his eyelids together, but the guard uses his meaty thumb to prise open his left eye. I squirm in my seat as he places the eye speculum over his left eye, wedging his eyelid into permanent openness.

"Now it's your turn to do the honors, Ruby," says Carlton, a small smile revealing his chiclet teeth that I'm beginning to dread. He only seems to smile when something horrific is happening.

My legs fail me the first time I try to stand up, but I realize what I have to do if I want to stay in this Program. I summon every piece of courage within my body and force myself to my feet and make my way to the front of the room. Dennis looks at me, a pleading expression in his one functioning eye, the other one darting around crazily as if trying to force itself into a blink.

Carlton calmly hands me the large tweezers. "Pluck, and then eat," he says, smiling at me. His eyes are dark, his pupils seeming to dance with excitement.

"Do I... do I get to at least cook the, um... eyeball?" The thought of what's about to happen is causing my stomach to churn. The anticipation of a gelatinous raw eyeball is almost too much to keep the contents of my stomach down.

"No. Think of it like a nice sashimi, if you will. You like sashimi, don't you, Ruby?"

"Yes, I do. But I mean... this is a person's eyeball. That's hardly the same as some sliced raw fish."

"Beggars can't be choosers, Ruby, as they say. And you're not in a position to question the rules now, are you? How badly do you want to graduate from this Program?"

"Badly," I say, softly, looking at Dennis in a way that I hope conveys my apology for what I'm about to do.

"Very well. Pluck, then eat. Or face the consequences."

"I'm so sorry, Dennis," I say as I lean forward and extend the tweezers so they grip onto his eyeball. He whimpers from beneath the gag as I clamp down firmly. I want this to be as quick and painless as possible for Dennis, and I want to get it over with.

I take a deep breath and count to three and then I yank as hard as I can. At first, I feel resistance, but then it gives way and my hand flies back. The tweezers pull out Dennis' eyeball, and the optic nerve is still attached. It looks like a bloody pink tail and I gag and retch at the sight.

"Do I—do I have to eat that part, too?" I say softly, pointing at the nerve.

"Oh yes. We don't believe in waste around here," shrugs Carlton. "We wouldn't want Dennis to go through all of this and then for you to waste his efforts now, would we?"

I gulp, my mouth suddenly feeling parched.

"Can I at least have some water?"

"Oh, of course. How rude not to offer you a beverage with your meal. Rocco?" Carlton gestures, and the guard exits and returns with a small cup of lukewarm water. It's better than nothing, and I've quickly learned to be grateful for the small things when it comes to this Program.

I try to tune out Dennis' ongoing whimpers, as well as the gasps and murmurs from around the room as the rest of the cohort looks on in horror.

I squeeze my eyes tightly shut and then shove the eyeball into my mouth and begin to chew. I was hoping to try to swallow it whole, but the surprise addition of Dennis' optic nerve is making it impossible. I retch but force myself to continue chewing, and use the water to gulp it down in several swallows.

Feeling disgusted with myself, I take one final sip of water and return to my seat, longing to remove the taste of eyeball and nerve from my mouth. Longing to pretend this never happened.

Who am I becoming? I know I can never come back from this.

"Oh my fucking god. What in the hell was that?" I try to keep my voice down, relying on the bubbling of the hot tub to dampen some of my volume.

"I'm trying so hard not to vomit right now. I didn't know that the eyeball had that... string thing attached. What even was that?!" yelps Erika.

I retch for what seems like the millionth time today. "Please don't remind me," I beg.

"And has anyone seen Dennis since it happened? After he got wheeled away?" Ryan glances around at each of us and we all shake our heads.

"I think they took him for urgent medical attention. I'm pretty sure his body was in shock. You should have seen his face up close," I say, blinking back tears. "I can't even imagine how his mind is beginning to process it. How his other eye will begin to adjust. Oh my god, I'm going to be sick. I can't believe I had to do that."

"Please don't...".

But it's too late. Vomit projects from my mouth, landing on the surface of the hot tub. We all scramble to get out before the chunks touch us. I grab a nearby striped towel and scrub my body furiously with it. It's not even about the vomit at this point. It's like I'm trying to scrub away the atrocities I've already seen and even participated in during my time here. And knowing the Program is only about halfway through is terrifying.

"I mean, how much more fucked up can this get? Are they going to start giving us lobotomies? Extracting part of our frontal lobes? Because at that point, I say fuck the consequences." Whitney's mouth is set in a thin line. She rubs my back as I regain my breath and wipe tears from my eyes.

"I don't think they would do that," I say, then I second-guess myself. "Then again, I never thought they'd do anything like this."

"Hey, think about what you just said," says Zach matter-of-factly. "It really could have been worse. He still has another eye. He can see. It's all you really need."

"*All you really need?* Do you hear yourself right now? That is complete insanity. You've reached the low point of justifying the most bizarre, horrific shit. Have some compassion, Zach."

"Yeah, fuck you, man," says Eugene.

The rest of the group towels themselves dry and we leave Zach next to the hot tub by himself, like a toddler who's been put in time out to think about what he's done.

It feels like this Program is changing us, just like we were told it would. But instead of an epic transformation that makes us better on the other end, I have a feeling that it's twisting us inside with the sharp blade of a knife. Desensitizing us. Causing some of us to justify the inhumane, the depraved, because we want so much to be the one or ones that make it through to the end.

It's bringing out the darkness, the worst in us. And I don't think this is something that can ever be reversed.

"Oh my fucking god. Can you believe that guy?" My nostrils flare and blood pounds in my temples.

"He's just saying what we're all thinking," shrugs Whitney. "To some degree it's becoming our mantra... *glad it's not us.*"

"It's going to be everyone's turn sometime soon. And god, if these tasks keep escalating maybe I should feel lucky I just got my turn out of the way."

"I understand your thinking, but I'd be careful. I feel like at some point our numbers are going to dwindle so hard that we're all going to be part of each and every task. There's not going to be anyone who can just sit back and be grateful and relieved they weren't selected this time around."

I shudder at the thought of having to participate in yet another—and worse, at that—challenge. "I wish they'd just tell us what they have planned so we can make an educated decision about whether we want to stay in the Program or not. If they gave us an idea of the potential consequences so we could weigh up our individual circumstances and make a choice. Although I have to say, after eating a human eyeball I'm feeling pretty invested. And pretty disgusting for it."

"But that would defeat the whole purpose of this aspect of the Program, wouldn't it? The complete mindfuckery of the unknown. Because the unknown is scary, and they clearly want to scare us."

"Does it really show strength just to go along with this whole thing without question, though? Maybe that's a test in itself. Maybe we'll be rewarded for being courageous."

"Oh, I don't think so. I have a ton of questions. I'm just not prepared to ask them right now."

"Why? Are you scared about what we've got ourselves into?"

"Yeah. I'm actually fucking terrified."

"So am I." I reach out and squeeze her shoulder in comfort. At least we have each other.

"I saw you with Ryan." There's a funny tone to Whitney's voice. She almost seems pissed, her facial expression unusually sullen and her arms crossed in front of her chest.

"Yeah, we were just chatting. Why? What's up?"

"Nothing." Her facial expression is pinched. Clearly something's up, but she's choosing not to be forthcoming. "He just seems like a douche, that's all."

"I mean, I got that vibe at first, too. But we've been chatting a bit more and I think it might just be a bit of a defense mechanism for him." I shrug. "He actually seems like a pretty cool guy, and I'm enjoying getting to know him. It's like one of the few positive things about this Program at the moment."

"Gee, thanks," she sneers.

"Jesus, Whitney," I exclaim. "What the hell has gotten into you? Clearly you are a big fat silver lining of this Program as well. There's no roomie I would rather have here. I couldn't do this whole thing without you."

"I guess... if I'm honest, I'm a bit jealous." She relaxes her shoulders slightly, her expression softening.

"But Whitney, we said the other night wasn't anything—."

She waves at me to stop. "No, not jealous like I want to be your girlfriend or anything lovey-dovey like that. But because you seem to be spending a lot of time with him. Time that we used to spend calming each other down about this ridiculous Program."

"Listen, I'm still here, Whit. I'll always be here. Any time you want to talk. Or cry. Or laugh. Or just shout 'why' at the sky in the middle of the night... I mean, figuratively, or we'd get kicked out of the Program for sure. But you know what I mean. I'm here. I'm still your girl."

"Are you sure?"

"One hundred percent."

"Okay. I forgive you then. Just don't forget about me."

"I could never."

CHAPTER FIFTEEN

*D*onovan

I've tried texting Ruby, but she hasn't replied. She always replies, usually straight away as if her phone is perpetually attached to her hand. But she's in that stupid Program I warned her about. I have no doubt that she had to turn her phone in when she got there. She wouldn't tell me where 'there' was, but I thankfully was keeping tabs on her and downloaded the address before she left, just in case. I shiver at the thought of her being unable to get in touch with anyone in the outside world, although at least she won't be able to text that Gerald idiot in a weak moment.

At the very least, I can keep her location information up my sleeve in case she ends up needing me. And I can use it for work as well, if it comes to that.

The rumors keep swirling about what goes on at this so-called Program. But nobody has ever made a formal complaint, so right now it's all just hearsay from a bunch of people with a vested interest in exchanging information to keep themselves out of jail or to minimize their time on the inside. Hardly reputable, I know. The order of reputable facts places criminal informants just under Wikipedia. Some of it's true, and a lot of it's not. But it doesn't mean I want Ruby being associated with any of that. She's been through too much already.

At this point, I think of myself as her guardian of sorts. Her family is pretty fucked up. Mostly non-existent, and the ones that do exist, well... let's just say they don't have her best interests at heart. So she was the perfect candidate for a Program like this. She sees herself as fierce—and she is, in many ways—but she's also incredibly vulnerable. The promise of a Program that can change her life once and for all, that would make her completely and utterly independent from anyone ever again—I can see the appeal for Ruby and why she refused to turn it down. It's the same reason I've seen so many vulnerable young people join gangs and work the city streets.

Besides, she's the most stubborn and headstrong person I've ever met in my life. So there's that, too.

But I have bigger fish to fry than the Program, right now. And these fish involve Ruby in a way that makes my stomach churn. I don't know how I'm going to find the right way to tell her.

Sure, part of my job is to pull up at family homes to tell parents that their child has died in a car crash, or to tell young parents that their elderly grandparent has been stabbed in a grocery store. Luckily I don't have to do that as much anymore, each instance firmly imprinted on my brain and occasionally showing up in nightmares. From time to time, I have to scrape brains and body parts off train tracks and roadways and work to identify the remains. There are parts of this job that truly traumatize me.

But there's been nothing like this. I dread telling Ruby that her already sad family life is about to be dealt another devastating blow.

A public one. One that I know she's going to take very personally. But she needs to know the truth.

And from someone she trusts, who truly cares about her.

She needs to hear it from me.

Chapter Sixteen

Ruby

"For this task, we've picked one of your nearest and dearest. And for those of you who draw the short straw, we're going to give you two options. The first is to choose for something harmful to happen to a loved one. You won't know what their fate will be, but I can promise it won't be good. Or, you can save your loved one, or at least have the opportunity to try to warn them and prevent the bad thing from happening. If you pick the second option, you of course will be eliminated from the program, but they will be saved. And then you'll face the consequences. You can think of this like a lose-lose, but you get to choose if it's you who loses or if it's them."

Carlton pulls a folded piece of paper out of the now-dreaded top hat. "Whitney! You're up first!"

Whitney's face pales and she looks around for a clue about what's about to happen.

"What will it be, Whitney? Warn them and drop out, or trust them to weather the storm?"

"Do I get any more information? Like who it is or what will happen to them?" Her voice trembles, her eyes darting wildly around the room as if someone else has the answers she needs to make her choice.

"Nope, we just need you to make your choice. The clock is ticking," says Carlton, his mouth pressed together in a creepy little duck-lipped smile.

"How could I possibly decide with no information?"

"If you're truly worthy of this Program, you'll trust your gut. So either drop out or let... let's call it nature... take its course."

"I, uh—," Whitney glances at me, her eyes large, clearly freaked out by the urgency with which she needs to make the decision. "I want to stay in the Program so I'll go with that option. Do what you need to do."

"*Do what you need to do*," Carlton's voice booms as he mimics her. "Most excellent, I was hoping you'd make that choice. Because it is *your* choice, Whitney. Everything that happens from hereon out is because of you. Rocco, play the feed."

The camera pans across the room, and an older lady is clearly visible sitting on an overstuffed couch bearing a floral pattern. She's holding knitting needles and expertly processing a ball of yarn. The camera quality is slightly pixelated, but clear enough to tell she has a slight tremor in her hands. Her long grey hair is tied back in a tight bun, and a fluffy ginger cat is nestled by her side. The TV emits a soft glow and the familiar faces of *The Golden Girls* concocting some harebrained scheme are clearly visible. She laughs at the screen, barely glancing down at her knitting. She's like everyone's stereotypical grandma, the one we all want and need in our lives.

"Oh my god!" Whitney shrieks, and her hand flies across her mouth. "That's my grandmother. Please don't hurt her! Anyone but her! She's old and doesn't deserve this!"

We look on in horror as a masked man appears on the screen.

"No, please! I'll do anything! Just please don't harm her!"

"You've made your decision already, Whitney. You know the rules. No takes-backsides." Carlton smirks at her, his eyes dancing with glee as the blood drains from her face.

"I thought it was just a test," whispers Whitney, her hand flying across her mouth. "I never think they'd actually harm people."

"I'm so sorry, Whitney," I whisper back. "I wish I could do something to help."

Everyone in the room looks on in horror as the masked man removes a scalpel and a small hammer from his jacket and proceeds to torture the kind-looking old lady. I flinch as her high-pitched cries and sobs echo through the parlor's surround sound system, and burst into tears as the masked man finally leaves her alone, crumpled on the ground.

Whitney leans over and vomits on the carpeted floor. She looks weak, but her eyes dart toward the door like she might run away at any moment. Not that anybody could blame her after what she just endured. Not that any of us could be blamed for fleeing after what we just saw.

"Are you having second thoughts about the program, Whitney?" asks Carlton. "Because by all means, feel free to leave. But you know what the consequences are."

The threat of the consequences again, now ever-present in our minds. If there's one thing I'm certain of, it's that the consequences would be worse than any actual challenge. Which is terrifying.

And after the last few tasks, I have no doubt they'll keep their word. They know so much, how to inflict the most pain. How to ruin lives completely.

It's clear that I'm going to be incredibly lucky to escape here with any shred of sanity. And now I'm beginning to wonder if I'm even going to make it out alive.

As if reading our minds, Carlton clears his throat. "Now, who's going to be next, I wonder?" He glances around at each of us individually and taking in all our facial expressions with perverse glee. He retrieves another piece of paper from the hat and grins as he reads the name to himself.

Nearly everyone shifts nervously in their chair, and when the camera changes to the view of the inside of another home, a man toward the back of the room whimpers. "Oh my god," he says, his entire body beginning to tremble. He's one of the older members of the group, someone I haven't really spoken with yet, but I think his name is Jensen. "That's my house."

What starts off as grainy aerial footage of a two-story suburban home comes into view. It's an attractive Cape Cod-style family home in what appears to be an upper-class suburban cul-de-sac, with a slated tile roof and a plethora of windows. The camera begins to pan into the wooden front door, zooming in on the vibrant yellow paint, almost as if we're being led into a virtual open house.

"You'll see we're taking some artistic license here," says Carlton. This time, he doesn't even try to hide the smile playing at the corners of his mouth and exposing his little teeth. "In fact, nothing ceases to surprise us, but this almost did."

Jensen squishes his brows together and frowns while looking upward at Carlton. "Wha—what do you mean?"

"You see, this sequence for this task has given us an... unexpected development... you might say. We're usually very prepared, but we weren't expecting this."

The camera almost toys with us as the picture fades out and appears to re-emerge inside the front entrance of the home. It's dark inside, but the picture is clear enough to make out that the home is clean and free from clutter, pleasantly decorated with the touches you might expect to see in a family home in a typical upper-income suburb.

"What's going on? Why are you taking us on a tour of my home? My family is sleeping."

"Are you sure they're sleeping, Jensen?"

"It's… it's like four o'clock in the morning over there. Of course they're sleeping. I don't understand." Jensen rubs the back of his neck and clears his throat.

Carlton smiles a cruel smile, gazing down his long, thin nose at the man who is visibly becoming increasingly agitated and confused by what's transpiring in his home.

"Are my children okay?"

"Oh yes, your children are sleeping soundly in their beds as we speak. For now at least. But there seems to be a commotion in one of the other rooms."

Jensen's face reddens, and a sheen begins to break out across his forehead, cheeks and chin.

"Which room?" His voice croaks, but by the way he looks down at his foot, one leg crossed over the other, and begins to jiggle it about, it's like he knows the answer and doesn't want to hear it out loud.

"Oh, your wife appears to be quite preoccupied in the master bedroom right now, Jensen." This time Carlton is unable to hold back a slight chuckle despite his usual unflappable poise.

"But I can tell this suspense is just about killing you, so we won't keep you waiting any longer. Jensen, switch to the master bedroom footage. Which is live. We found something unexpected when we entered the premises. Although maybe it's not that unexpected, considering…". His gaze turns to Jensen once more, and it's teeming with judgement.

The camera then switches to another room, and it is clearly very much a master bedroom. A large king-sized bed takes center stage in the back center of the room, nightstands with lamps flanking the large rectangle.

We all lean forward, even though the screen is plenty big enough for all of us to see in crystal clear detail what's going on in there.

Expecting to see what I anticipate to be an attractive, middle-aged woman tucked up in her bed, instead we are greeted with something entirely unanticipated. A very muscular, and quite attractive I might say, ass. Belonging to a man. A man who is quite clearly plowing the shit out of a woman in the bed. The back side of the man thrusts rapidly back and forth as the man rails the woman from behind.

We all turn to Jensen as the color drains from his face and his mouth falls open, his eyes beginning to bulge and rapidly blink. His eyes are glued to the screen.

"Turn on the audio, Rocco. Pull out all the stops for Jensen, here."

The burly guard obliges, pressing a button which immediately turns the room from one of silent shock to what sounds like a surround sound porn set.

The loud moans of the woman fill the room, and she cries out each time the man thrusts into her. At first I wonder if we've stumbled on some type of attack, but then her words ring out clear as day. "Oh, yeah, fuck the shit out of me, daddy! Give me that giant cock!"

My hand flies over my mouth as I realize what's happening. Everyone's eyes once again fly to Jensen.

He's visibly sweating now, his nostrils flaring and his lip beginning to curl.

"Given this... interesting development... we'd like to give you an option, Jensen," says Carlton. "You see, we were planning on giving your wife the, uh... full treatment, same as Whitney's grandmother just before. But…" he pauses, "it looks like somebody's already taking care of that."

Jensen's face grows more flushed and mottled by the moment, turning from an unattractive red to an even more angry purple. His neck starts to cord and after what seems like an intense internal struggle, he manages to glance at Carlton.

"Given what we've found, we want to give you another option. We can… take care of this little… situation for you, if you prefer. You'll be able to watch, of course. Think of it as a two-for-one special. A buy-one-get-one- free deal… what do they call that in retail stores these days? BOGO?"

Our host's flippancy seems to simultaneously piss Jensen off further and also capture his attention.

"You mean…"

"Oh yes, by 'take care of' we would be more than happy to murder your wife and her lover, if you wish. Our treat to you in the circumstances. Just say the word, and your wish is our command. All we insist upon is that you and the rest of this group has to watch every moment of it."

Jensen glances back at the television.

"How—who is he? Do you know how long this has been going on for?"

"Oh yes. We weren't expecting to find them together tonight, but it seems that your wife actively solicited this man's attention online, and he was more than happy to comply. In fact, it's been going on for some months now. Every time you're at work, he comes over to…fix her plumbing, you might say. She's very complimentary about his skills as a lover. Can't stop raving about his prowess or the size of his enormous member."

Spittle has built up in the corner of Jensen's mouth, and if he turns any more purple, he's going to resemble an iconic character from a fast-food restaurant or a human eggplant emoji.

His lips retract, baring his teeth and he lets out a guttural roar. "KILL THEM!"

"Are you sure?" asks Carlton calmly. "Of course you can't change your mind."

"KILL THEM!!" Jensen roars. "MAKE IT HURT!"

"Okay," Carlton smiles, his dark eyes dancing under the overhead light. "I was hoping you'd say that." He turns to the man operating the cameras. "Radio the team and let them know to go ahead with Plan B."

Whitney and I turn to each other, our eyes wide, and without speaking I reach out a hand and she takes it as we look on.

Three men in balaclavas rush into the bedroom, and as the man turns to look he pulls out of the woman, leaving her gaping asshole exposed to the camera.

Despite the intruders, the sight of his wife only serves to enrage Jensen further, and he roars again.

He looks on intently, unblinking, as the masked men pull out large, shiny blades. They begin with the man on the bed, two of the intruders holding his large body down while the third stabs him in the back repeatedly. He thrashes about wildly, but he's no match for the Program's hit team. Blood splatters everywhere from the walls to the sheets, including over the woman, as he's stabbed over and over again. She hugs her arms closely to her chest, rocking slightly, her eyes wide in what appears to be a combination of dread and disbelief. Her pale flesh is streaked with scarlet splatters and spots of her lover's blood. So much blood that the streaks are running together and dripping down her face, her torso and her limbs.

The man's body finally stops jerking, and he stills. The masked men roll him off the bed, discarding him as if he's an incidental obstacle that just happened to be in the way. Only his lower half is visible in the camera's lens now, his very naked, very dead body on display for the room to observe.

Jensen clenches his fists together as two of the men approach his wife, grabbing her by each arm. By now, she's scrunched herself up at the head of the bed, her knees tucked against her body. She lets out a bloodcurdling shriek as the third man hops onto the bed in front of her and wields the bloody knife and points it directly at her face. She winces as she tries to twist her neck out of the way so the sharp tip of the blade gets further from her eyeballs. He raises it above his head and brings it down, slicing her open throughout her torso, and she lets out another blood-curdling scream. Eventually the shrieks stop, and blood oozes from her mouth as she collapses dead on the bed, her eyes rolling back and an eerie death rattle emanating from her throat.

"There you go," says Carlton nonchalantly, as if the men just knocked off the most simple of household chores. "Done and dusted. Are you happy now, Jensen?"

Jensen retches in his seat. He then falls off his chair and into the fetal position, and lets out a loud sob. His facial expression grows slack, his chest seeming to sink on itself as he begins to rock back and forth. He places his hands over his face as he continues to sob. "Oh god. Oh god, no. What have I done?"

"Now, now," says Carlton, his voice growing icy. "No need to be pathetic. We just gave you exactly what you wanted."

He glances up at the screen, at the body of his very dead wife and that of her muscular lover with the giant cock which now lies flaccid against his abdomen. The guy was a shower not a grower, for sure.

Jensen howls in agony as, to our horror, a couple of small children come running into the room. They're both boys, and the oldest can't be more than about six years old. The contrast of their matching dinosaur pajamas and the bloody corpses of their mother and her lover is disarming.

"Mommy, mommy!" they yell, as they notice their mother covered in stab wounds, lying on the now-red sheets.

"No... not the children." Jensen's voice dips low, and he looks on in horror as the intruders murder his innocent children. Thankfully, they show mercy and make it quick with point-blank shots to the forehead. Those poor boys. I hope they felt no pain.

Jensen lets out a guttural howl and begins to sob. His body wracks and he tries to look away, but his gaze keeps returning to the screen.

"How could you kill... my children?" he whispers.

"You seemed quite supportive of this task, Jensen. You don't get to make the rules here. And there are always, always consequences. You can't have everything your way. Unless you make it to the end of this Program, of course."

Jensen's face flashes with rage, but then he begins to sob again. It's like he's so beaten down by what he just saw, and by his role in it, that he knows getting aggressive would just be futile. It's definitely not going to bring them back, that's for sure.

"Rocco, take Jensen to his room seeing he's being pitiful. In the circumstances, he won't be subject to immediate elimination, but he will need to pull himself together and quickly in order to be eligible to continue with the program."

The security team obliges, two of the men taking the still-sobbing Jensen by each arm and ushering him out of the viewing room and in the direction of his bedroom.

Whitney looks at me, her eyes large. "I think I'm going to be sick," her face as drained of color as I imagine my own is right now.

"Me too," I whisper, realizing we're still holding hands and I squeeze hers in an attempt to comfort her as well as myself. "I can't believe they harmed the children. His entire family gone, because of the Program." She squeezes mine back.

"Now, I think we've all earned a bit of a break after that, don't you?" It's yet another rhetorical statement from Carlton, but several people nod. Looking around the room, everyone seems a few shades paler than normal, except for Erika and Eugene who look strangely excited. It's like they're even a little turned on by what happened. I wonder if they're going to use the much-needed break time to jerk off in their rooms.

"Wow, this Program is really heating up. I'm starting to believe it's the real deal!" Ryan's eyes are bright with excitement. He looks exhilarated, like he just got off the most thrilling roller coaster of his life.

"What is wrong with you?!" My voice is octaves higher than usual, because I can't believe what's coming out of his mouth.

"Whatever do you mean?"

"We just watched a grandmother attacked in her own home while she was knitting, for god's sakes. And then we watched a family get massacred while the supposed head of the household looked on and *encouraged* it because he was sick with jealousy."

"Well, let's just say today has removed all doubts about whether this Program is made-up or if it really can change the lives of the people who make it through. I'm confident I will. And it's a trip seeing how this all plays out in the process!"

"A *trip*? Watching people be killed is a *trip* to you? Witnessing the devastation of their loved ones as they look on? Seeing how much this is affecting all of us, and fucking with our heads? You had a finger chopped off, and I had to eat a man's fucking eyeball, Ryan!"

He snickers. "Now, now. You're overreacting. I thought you were made of stronger stuff, that you were in this program for a reason. I'm starting to think they might have picked you out by accident. And I'd be careful about what you say, Ruby. You know that talking negatively about the program is grounds for being removed, or facing a consequence. You seem to be against the tasks and the consequences. So maybe you should do us all a favor and remove yourself."

"Fuck. You." I'm seething, and I can feel my nostrils flare, my eyes locked upon his. If there was ever an example of human filth that should be lobotomized to perform hard labor for the rest of his life, it's this guy. What a sack of shit. Funny that I ever thought he was attractive, because he's turned out to be a complete dick. Probably could subconsciously read that about him from the first time I met him. Given my track record, that would make sense.

**

I return to my room and spend the next two hours seething after my interaction with Ryan earlier. The words that came out of his mouth are unforgivable, and served to erase any pleasant moments between us.

"You okay?" asks Whitney, finally, having steered clear of me up until now. "I just had an argument with Ryan," I sniff.

"Wanna talk about it? Because I'm here to listen." She smiles softly, the jealousy from the other day seeming to have dissipated.

I sigh. "I think the bottom line is that I can't trust anyone."

"Tell me more."

"Well, people try to pop back into my life from time to time because it makes them feel wanted or needed or just there or whatever. But the truth is they all fucking suck. They all have an angle. I'm there for them. Or I am someone who is just there. I don't know. But it's honestly just shit. I feel like I'm falling into a black hole and the sides are a giant tall tunnel filled with mud ten times my height and I keep trying to rake myself out of it. And sometimes I have managed to like twenty times without assistance, but at the end of it the sides are just muck and I keep sliding downward. And they keep trying to help me but it's just fake, fake, fake. And I get swept away into the filth. Like nothing I said ever mattered. And maybe it doesn't. Even though I wanted it to so much."

Whitney walks over and wraps her arms around me. I appreciate that she didn't try to interrupt.

"Thank you for being here. You're a good listener." I hug her back.

But even though this moment is sweet and I have a friend for now, nobody will ever be there in the way I truly need ever again.

I need to face that I'm broken. I'm crushed. I tried to start anew and got pounded down again several times. Maybe I'm just meant to be down here.

It's not just my body.

It's my heart, my mind, my soul.

And nobody can ever fix that. Even me.

Chapter Seventeen

Ruby

"Are you okay?" I put my arm around Whitney's shoulder and squeeze her while we sit side-by-side on my bed.

"No, I'm not okay. I don't think any of us are anymore, after the last couple of days. But I don't want to talk about what happened with my grandma. Please. I can't do anything about it. I just have to hope she's in good hands."

"Are you sure? That was horrific."

"Yeah, it was. But if I think about it too much more, I am going to lose my mind. I feel incredibly guilty, but also I didn't really have much of a choice, no matter what Carlton says."

"I'm not judging you," I say, softly. "You didn't have enough information to know what would happen. Whoever would have thought they would go and terrorize someone's family, let alone an elderly grandmother? They're clearly sick fucks. But I don't know what's scarier. To stay in the Program or leave. I get the feeling we're fucked either way." I turn to hug Whitney with both arms and she returns the hug, pressing her head into my shoulder. After a few moments, she lifts her head up and looks at me, a mischievous look beginning to play over her face.

"You know, I was a little petrified by what happened earlier as it was happening. But then the more I thought about it, I realized it was kind of sexy."

I give Whitney a sideways look. "Sexy, how? They killed his wife and family... I don't think that sounds like a turn-on."

"Yeah, but it was kind of poetic, you know?" Her face takes on a dreamy expression, her eyes softly hooded with a slowly spreading smile. "Here Jensen is, going through the effort to get to the end of the Program which would change his family's life for the better. And she's over there whoring around while he tries to provide for them. It seems only fitting that she gets her just desserts."

"You think she deserved to die because of that?"

"Well, what other punishment would fit the crime, Rubes? Tickle torture? Because it looked like that guy was already tickling her with his big old dick."

I look at her in shock. How can she be so ruthless?

"Look, come on. Stop being such a prude." She grabs my hand and pulls me closer. "You're clearly still a little ruffled by what you just saw. Let me distract you."

I'm feeling quite tipsy by now, the wine creating a pleasant buzz in my brain. My senses are softened, and I'm enjoying the numb feeling that's distracting me. Whitney's hand is soft on mine, and I can't help but notice how pretty she is. Sexy, even.

Her long brown hair with blonde highlights cascades over her shoulders, the ends hitting the tops of her curved breasts that glow under the gentle golden light of the night lamp beside my bed. I admire how her eyes twinkle in the light, her plump lips curved upward in a cheeky smile. Her nipples protrude seductively through her tank top which barely covers her flat midriff. And her shorts are tight, revealing strong thighs and leading to shapely calves and feet with hot pink toenail polish.

"I—haven't been with a girl before," I say, little butterflies jiggling in my stomach. "Not that I haven't thought about it. The opportunity just hasn't come up yet."

"Well, I have," she smirks at me, "and I enjoy it. I can show you what to do."

She straddles me, pressing my body against the headboard. The protruding metal sticks into my back but I don't mind as she spreads my legs open beneath her, causing her own to open wide above me. She gently rubs herself against me, and my pussy clenches as I feel some of her wetness as it drips onto me.

Tentatively at first, I wrap my arms around her neck. She responds by pulling herself closer to me, causing our breasts to rub against hers. Our nipples are rock hard, and the friction causes ripples of pleasure to rocket from my breasts to my core. Her hips roll against mine and I reciprocate, creating a pleasant rhythm between us. She mashes her lips against mine, our teeth clashing as our tongues hungrily explore each other.

She pulls me further down on the bed and kisses her way down my body. Little flickers of pleasure radiate throughout my body as she sucks each of my nipples into her mouth one at a time, swirling her tongue as she gently bites down. She continues to trail kisses down my torso until she reaches my thighs, which she pushes further apart and buries her head between.

Wasting no time, she licks me. I moan as her tongue laps at my clit. I've had my pussy eaten before, many times, but this is different. It's like she knows exactly what I need. She's soft but aggressive at the same time and it's perfect. I moan as her tongue dips into my pussy, tasting me, and again as she drags the flat of her tongue back up to my clit and sucks it into her mouth.

I grind my hips against her mouth and she increases the pace of her tongue as it flicks against me.

Before I can even register what's happening, the orgasm smashes through me and my legs wrap around her head, pulling her close. She continues to lash me as I ride out my peak until I have nothing left. I'm ultra-sensitive now, and she giggles as I squirm against her tongue that continues to work my clit. I try to push her away but she just clenches me closer to her face, as if daring me to ride out a second orgasm.

Feeling relaxed but also intrigued by this interaction and still horny, I turn the tables. I pull Whitney up to me and explore her mouth with my own. She tastes like my pussy, and I enjoy tasting myself on her as our tongues lash against each other.

I reach down and caress her wet pussy with my fingers, dipping my fingers inside her entrance and feeling her soft wetness. She's soaking, and I like that I'm the reason for it. I become the aggressor now, flipping her over on her back, and I enjoy seeing her hooded eyes darken with lust as she realizes it's her turn to receive pleasure. I remove my mouth from hers and she tilts her neck back as I trail kisses down her throat and make my way down her chest. I stop at her gorgeous breasts, sucking one of her nipples into my mouth and cupping my hand against the other. She moans and arches her back as I flick my tongue against her rock-hard peak. I continue to make my way down her body, enjoying the feel of her soft, smooth flesh against my lips. I enjoy the feeling of the soft swell of her stomach and continue my way down until my face reaches her pussy.

She moans as she feels my breath against her, and I tease her by gently brushing my mouth against her clit before moving to her entrance. I want to taste her, to explore every inch of her.

While I haven't done this before, I'm attuned to how her body is responding. I know what I enjoy, and while I don't expect her to crave and respond to the same things in the exact same way, it at least gives me a place to start.

She moans with pleasure as I trail my tongue from her entrance up to her clit and keep my focus there, licking her swollen bud with slow, languid strokes. I'm not in a rush. I just want to make her feel good. It's enjoyable, the feel of her soft velvety smoothness against my tongue. I could get used to this. Don't get me wrong. I enjoy dick. But the sensation of her pussy against my tongue is making me feel things I didn't know I was capable of. And her intoxicating scent. It's hard to describe, but the way she tastes and her scent are doing things to me I never thought possible. I just came, and I'm already craving more.

I continue to lap at her clit and she rhythmically grinds her hips, raising her knees up as if to open herself up to me. She moans again as I slide two of my fingers inside of her, feeling her walls as they clench against me while I slide in and out of her. I use the flat of my tongue to maximize the surface area as I lick her, and then I extend it into a firm point which I use to flick against her clit. She's breathing heavily now, panting even, and I can tell she's close.

"Fuck, Ruby. When did you learn to eat pussy?"

"Just now," I respond, my heart racing. Am I good enough for her?

"You're a fucking beast," she rasps. "Keep going. Please."

I continue to lap my tongue against her glistening pussy, focusing on her clit while she grinds against my face. I slide two fingers inside her and they glide in easily, her tight entrance slick with arousal. She moans as I slide my fingers in and out rapidly as I continue to focus my tongue on her clit.

"Fuck, I'm so close," she cries, and I feel her body tense, her back arching. From between her thighs, I admire the way her rock-hard nipples tilt toward the ceiling, her gorgeous breasts reflecting the gentle light from the bedside lamp.

Her hips buck, and she wraps her legs around my head. I feel her pussy pulse around my fingers as her orgasm crests, and she crushes her pussy against my mouth while she rides it out, her juices flowing. I lap them up eagerly, enjoying the intoxicating way she tastes.

Without taking a pause, Whitney flips herself on top of me and turns me onto my back. She lifts my arms above my head and presses down on my forearms, holding me still while she dips her mouth to meet mine. She slides her tongue inside, tasting herself. "Mmm, you taste like me," she says as I kiss her back, forcefully exploring and wrestling her tongue with my own.

We eventually fall asleep tangled in one another's limbs. At some point, I wake and notice she's returned to her own bed. She's softly snoring, and I can make out the gentle rise and fall of her chest.

This day definitely wasn't how I expected it to be. Whitney's definitely a great distraction, and I enjoyed our playtime together. I just hope things don't get awkward, especially since we're roommates. Besides, I'm not looking for anything serious. I just hope she feels the same way.

"Hey sleepyhead." She smiles at me and rubs her eyes.

"Hey you," I smile back, feeling a flicker of trepidation. *Please don't let things be weird. Please don't let things be weird.*

"Last night was....". She pauses. Oh god, here it comes. I quirk my brow and try to stay calm, but my heart is starting to race. "I enjoyed it, but I'm worried this is going to make things weird between us. I think we should just keep it to... whatever it was. And focus on being friends so we can make it out of here."

Relief courses through me and I let out the breath I was apparently holding. "Oh yes, absolutely. I was thinking the same thing. The last thing we need is for things to get weird between us. There's enough weird shit going down in this place without us needing to add to it."

She laughs, also seeming relieved. "You can say that again. Not that it means I would be against a repeat. That was fucking intense."

I smile back at her. "I feel the same way."

Chapter Eighteen

R *uby*

We return to meet the group at the appointed time.

I wonder if they can tell that my mouth tastes like pussy. Whitney's pussy.

I brushed my teeth three times and used mouthwash, just in case. Not that I'm embarrassed or ashamed by what happened. But I just don't need the group talking about this. It's fresh for me. And I don't want to get in trouble or be doled out punishment for some hidden rule that I didn't know about. Nobody said anything about not being able to fuck your roommate, but I wouldn't put it past this group to make a big deal about it and use it against us. To try to get us 'thrown off the island', so to speak.

I told Whitney about my concerns and she laughed it off.

"For all we know, Zach and Eugene have been off in their room playing hide the sausage," she'd said, which made me snort at the time. The thought of Zach's bulky frame superimposed against Eugene's string-bean like appearance is comical, even though I'd have no problem with it if it made them both happy.

She's right. What happens behind closed doors should be nobody else's business. But here, it seems that everything that happens is everyone's business. Especially for the people who run the Program.

They've made it clear that they are more than prepared to use information against us. To destroy lives. And so my lapse in judgement in sleeping with someone—doesn't matter what gender they are—during this Program, makes me want to slap myself silly. There's so much at stake here, and no amount of pussy or dick should be worth compromising that for.

Shame on me.

Maybe Eugene and Clark were both right about me.

Maybe I deserve what's happened to me in the past, and what's destined for my future.

What a fucking whore.

CHAPTER NINETEEN

Ruby

"For our next task, we're going to get to know each other a little better," says Carlton. "Well, a lot better. And when I say 'we', I mean you."

"I'd say we've gotten to know each other pretty well already, wouldn't you say?" Zach smirks. For the love of god, I wish I had a zipper that I could attach to his mouth to keep it permanently closed.

"You're going to be blindfolded, and you're going to get to know someone in this group rather intimately. You won't know who it is. You'll be wearing earplugs so the sounds won't give it away. The rest of the group will observe."

What in the actual fuck? Does this mean what I think it means?

"You mean… we're going to have sex with someone else in this group but we won't know who it is?" Ryan speaks up and asks what we're all wondering. He sounds a little perplexed, but there's a hint of what could be arousal in his tone as well.

"Well, exactly what you get up to is up to you, of course. We'd never force you to do anything you're uncomfortable with. But yes, the expectation is that there is some degree of intimacy between the people who are grouped together. Besides, we are well aware that some of you have decided to engage in these types of activities already." Carlton looks around the room, giving several people pointed glances.

Whitney and I make brief eye contact and then quickly look away. I glance up at the camera in the corner of the room. I haven't seen one in our bedroom, but I wouldn't put it past the Crew to have hidden some cameras discreetly away in everyone's sleeping quarters to keep an eye on us. For all I know, they watched Whitney and I and know exactly what we got up to last night.

Oh well, let them watch.

We don't have anything to be embarrassed about.

I feel a hand on my thigh. Goosebumps form as I feel the hand slide tentatively up my leg until a finger hooks into my panties and brushes against me. I can feel myself getting wet. There's something thrilling about not knowing who this hand belongs to. From its roughness and its sheer size, I can tell it's a man. But which man?

I'm really hoping it's Ryan. I haven't been able to stop thinking about him. Still blindfolded, I try to think back to what any of the men's hands in our group look like. To what they might feel like. But I guess they're not something I tend to focus on or record in my brain.

The hand pulls my panties down roughly, and I feel a finger trail against my slit. I'm scared, but also turned on at the thought of who this might be. My encounter with Whitney was satisfying and I can't stop thinking about it. It feels like anything is possible sexually here, and the mystery of this challenge, while unusual, has me feeling aroused.

I gasp as the rough finger that traced its way along my pussy is suddenly replaced by the feeling of a warm tongue. It begins to lap at me and I involuntarily begin to grind my hips in rhythm as it continues to lick me along my slick folds, and then begins to focus on my clit. I feel a soft hum coming from the person as they lick me, unable to hear their voice but feeling its depth as it vibrates against my clit. In this moment, I suddenly don't mind who is doing this to me, because whoever they are they're certainly good at it.

I feel my ear plugs being removed.

"Alright, now. Everyone has been grouped and the activities have commenced. You may now remove your blindfolds." I pause for one second, almost too afraid to see what's going on both to me and around me. But then I can't hold back and I quickly untie it. *Please be Ryan. Please be Ryan.*

But it's not Ryan. The man feasting on my pussy is Zach.

The frat bro that I can't seem to escape.

The mousy girl, Erika, is suddenly not so mousy anymore. Her breasts bounce as she slams her pussy down on Ryan's cock. I can hear her wetness as she impales herself on his girthy shaft over and over again. She cups her breasts and massages her nipples as she rides him, letting out moans every time he plows deep into her. I've never been so jealous in my life as I watch her riding the incredibly hot man. And she's clearly enjoying this, as if it's empowering her to show off her femininity while she dominates his cock.

Whitney straddles his face, and I watch as his tongue expertly works her clit. She grinds against him, her eyes rolling back in her head as she tilts her head back, exposing her throat. He holds her hips as she bucks against his face, and I moan as Zach's tongue laps at my clit and I watch Ryan's tongue continuing to pleasure Erika. I can't help but pretend it's Ryan's tongue flicking against my own clit. Don't get me wrong, Zach is pretty good at eating pussy. But I want so badly for it to be Ryan flattening his tongue against my swollen bud. I want it to be Ryan trailing his tongue down to my arousal-coated entrance and sliding it inside my pussy, in and out, tongue fucking me.

Ryan slides his hands up and cups Whitney's breasts in his hands as he continues to devour her. I glance up at Whitney and see her gaze fixated on Zach's tongue as he laps at my pussy. Lust fills her eyes as she continues to ride Ryan's face. Erika continues to slam herself down on his cock.

She bucks her hips and begins to thrash wildly on his cock as she reaches orgasm.

Zach is on top of me now, and as he lines himself up with my entrance, I'm pleasantly surprised to feel his hard girth against me. The way he acted, I would have figured him to be compensating for a tiny penis with his larger-than-life, won't-shut-the-fuck-up personality. But his cock is large, too. Interesting. I wonder how many other obnoxious guys I've underestimated in that department.

He glides into me easily and proceeds to rail the living shit out of me. I cry out as his cock stretches my walls. I glance over as Ryan orgasms, his strong arms grabbing Erika's hips tightly as he releases inside of her. His head tilts back in ecstasy, but his eyes stay firmly fixed on me.

It's enough to send me over the edge and my pussy convulses wildly around Zach's cock, my hips bucking wildly beneath him. It's enough to send him into his own orgasm, and I feel him pumping into me while my eyes remain locked with Ryan's.

We all lay there, spent, gradually remembering we're not the only ones in the room.

"Very well," says Carlton. "You have all passed the challenge. Congratulations. You have made it onto the next stage."

We all put our clothing back on again and return to our seats. I desperately need a shower, but I don't dare push my luck by asking Carlton. There must be a break coming up soon.

"Wow, that was... something," whispers Whitney. "Are you okay?"

"Hey, it could have been way worse," I whisper back. "As far as challenges go, it's my favorite one so far."

"Yeah, let's just hope you didn't get pregnant. Can you imagine that? Having Zach as your baby daddy? You'd be stuck with him for life. And your baby would probably pop out with a giant Zach-sized bobblehead."

I cringe at the thought. "Don't even joke about that! I couldn't bear it."

"Were you jealous?" Ryan stands next to me at the line for dinner. It's a self-service buffet this time, with yet another delectable selection of steaks and fish and colorful vegetables. He smirks at me, and I want to punch him in the face. Sort of.

"No." I jut out my bottom lip.

"You're lying."

"Okay," I shrug. "Maybe I was a little jealous."

"How jealous?" His eyes twinkle. He's teasing me. Two can play this game.

"Extremely." I lock eyes with him.

He quirks an eyebrow. "Oh yeah? Why?"

"You really want to know? I wanted it to be me that was slamming myself down on your big cock. I wanted to be the one riding your face."

He looks shocked but also quite pleased, and I swear his pants begin to strain slightly in his crotch region. "Did it turn you on, watching me fuck those girls?"

"I've definitely touched myself thinking about it. I'm sure I'll have dreams about it tonight. Why? Did you enjoy watching Zach and me?"

He smirks. "I didn't take him for your type."

I laugh. "Oh he's definitely not."

"Well, you certainly seemed to be enjoying yourself."

"Turns out he has a nice cock, and he knows how to eat pussy. So as far as people I could have been partnered with, considering I couldn't get my first choice...".

"Now you're making *me* jealous."

"Well, if you want to know the truth, the whole time, I was imagining that it was your tongue. That I was the one riding your cock and your face."

"Oh yeah? Well, I was imagining your pussy. All I could think about is how you taste, how you smell. How it would feel to be inside you."

"So I don't have anything to worry about?" I arch an eyebrow.

"What? Like a repeat with those girls?"

"Yeah."

"No, you have absolutely nothing to worry about. That was just a task for me. Did it feel good? Yeah, it felt fucking good. But all I could think about was you."

Chapter Twenty

R uby

The Next Day

We've been given a free pass to relax, and most of us have enjoyed a lazy day by the pool. I've spent a decent amount of time in the hot tub, listening to music and enjoying the usual selection of refreshing beverages and snacks. Despite the horrors of the challenges we've endured, days like this remind us that the Program can give us access to opportunities we can only dream of.

At dinner time, we make our way down to the grand dining hall to another sumptuous spread. This time, tureens full of a savory broth are placed in the middle of the table, and we eagerly ladle the meaty stew into large, fine china bowls. Sitting in the hot tub all day has made me work up quite an appetite, and I take a substantial amount of the mouthwatering dish for myself. Servers come around and crack pepper into our bowls with tall, ornate pepper grinders. They also offer each of us little plates of garlic croutons, freshly shaved parmesan cheese and fresh herbs to sprinkle on top in the amounts we prefer.

"Let's dig in. This looks heavenly," says Ryan.

We all nod and take spoonfuls of the rich, meaty broth.

"Oh my god, this is to die for!" exclaims Whitney, and several others nod, including me. It's savory and umami and just the most indescribably delectable flavor I've ever experienced.

For once, the dining room is in relative silence, everyone deeply focused on savoring their stew. The only noises are the clinking of spoons against bowls and the occasional slurping noise as everyone enthusiastically devours their meal.

"Has anybody seen Zach?" Eugene asks, glancing around the table.

"Not for a while," says Georgina. "Haven't heard him either, which is surprising. Besides, he's normally the first one here for meals. It's his favorite part of the day." Several of us smirk at the accuracy.

"Oh, Zach is here," Carlton's voice rings out from behind us, his amusement at this announcement palpable in his tone. "I do hope you're enjoying him."

The room hushes and I lock eyes with Ryan. Everyone looks down at their plates in unison.

I consider the richness of the beef broth, the way the meat was marbled and sinewy.

"You don't mean—," gasps Eugene.

"Oh, I most certainly do," Carlton pinches his lips together in his creepy, thin-lipped smile.

Several of us start to retch as we realize we're eating a frat boy.

"Now, now. Zach worked out so hard, he was like a Wagyu beef on the inside. Perfectly marbled. That's why he's so tender despite his muscularity."

Eugene immediately loses the contents of his stomach, and it's enough for several of us to start heaving.

Carlton merely smiles and clasps his fingers together.

"Come, now," he says. "You all needed a spot of healthy protein. And I can assure you that you don't want to do anything to offend our chef. He's a wizard when it comes to knives and fire, after all."

As if on cue, the burly chef emerges from the kitchen wielding a large chef's cleaver that sparkles in the dimly lit dining hall. He smiles at us warmly. "Good evening, Cohort! I trust you're enjoying your very special meal this evening?"

He notices the bile and vomit that Eugene couldn't hold back from expelling from his body and a shadow passes over his face. "What? You didn't like?" He gestures at the mess.

"I, uh—", says Eugene meekly. "I just had a bit of an upset stomach all day, really. Nothing to do with your food."

Still brandishing the cleaver, the chef approaches him. "Are you sure? Would you like to come out back so I can make you something else?"

"No, no. I'm quite alright, thank you. Really."

"Okay then. I'll bring you another bowl. We have a little left over. The carcass we were working with was... quite large."

Eugene gulps and breathes an almost audible sigh of relief as the Chef retreats into the kitchen. He quickly returns with a full bowl, this larger than the last.

"I love watching people enjoy my creations," he beams. His voice rises. "Now EAT."

He watches like a hawk as we continue to shovel bites of the rich, fatty meat into our mouths. Luckily there's a glass of water in front of me and I gulp at it between mouthfuls.

I'm embarrassed and ashamed that I was enjoying this meal... until I knew what it was. The meat was tender, a little gamey, but perfectly complimented by the rich, dark gravy that Chef and his team expertly prepared.

Now my heartbeat races in my chest and my mouth feels bone-dry. For someone that was hungry bordering on hangry only moments ago, my appetite has well and truly left the building and I feel like I may never eat again.

Zach was annoying, but I never would have chosen him for dinner or any other meal. I'd never thought about what human flesh would taste like, but I guess now I know. And I'm disgusted with myself for savoring the flavor before its ingredients were disclosed.

The air hangs silent in the cavernous dining space, except for the clang of the ladle against the large ceramic soup tureen as Chef makes another round, topping up each of our soup bowls wit more of the chunky man stew. Scrapes of spoons against our dishes, and the odd chewing sound as one of us attempts to force down the now-horrific meal prepared especially for us.

My mind flashes back to the sound of porridge-like slop being ladled into breakfasts bowls at the boarding school I briefly attended while I was growing up. It was colorless, flavorless, and made with a complete absence of love. It tasted like desperation and pain. We were made to force down the stodgy concoction as quickly as possible each day, and I dreaded it from the moment I woke up each morning. "Be grateful," my mother would chide me and my siblings if any of us dared to complain, and even if we didn't. "Not everybody gets a hot meal in the morning. Eat up now or you can go to your room without any breakfast, and won't be allowed out until dinner time." She would smirk as each of us tried to gulp down the lumpy, anemic mess. I swear she took pride in making it as flavorless and unappetizing as possible, sometimes adding unspecified ingredients to make it more unpleasant. As I look at the dwindling contents of the bowl before me, trying to force down each chunk of meat without hurling, I can hear her voice cackling in my head at the thought of me being forced to eat a bowl of human flesh. What I would give for another bowl of that disgusting breakfast slop in place of the horrific meal before me. And I hate that I feel this way. Because I know that it would only serve to please her.

The thought of it almost makes me wretch again, but I inhale deeply and take another large gulp of water as I feel Chef's eyes wandering over me, and breathe the air slowly out my nose. I look up and smile, giving him a thumb's up and he beams back at me. All I know is I don't want to be the person who finishes my plate last or first, and I definitely don't want to show signs of the revulsion that bubbles away inside of me. My mind focuses only on taking long, deep breaths through my nose, ignoring the aroma of the dish that sits in front of me. I don't want to risk a consequence for offending Chef, and I definitely don't want him to think I love the dish so much that he insists on giving me another steaming bowl of Zach. Frat bro soup for dinner. Oh my god.

I toss and turn all night, my mind full of nightmares involving rotting corpses and decaying frat bros. At one point, I wake up in a panic. I'm covered in sweat and my head is pounding. It was a dream about cannibalism, and for an instant when I wake up I'm incredibly relieved that it was only a nightmare. But just as quickly, I'm brought back down to earth as I realize we really did eat another human being for dinner.

Glancing over at Whitney, I see she's awake as well. "You doing okay?"

"Yeah. Well, relatively speaking. I didn't get served up to this group on an actual platter, so I feel like I'm ahead of the game."

"Yeah, things really do seem to be going sideways. These people are depraved. Twisted. I'm not sure what they could possibly dream up next, and I'm not sure I want to know. But I also know that I don't have a choice. We need to get through to the end of this."

"Do you think you're going to be able to live with yourself if you do?"

"What do you mean?"

"I mean, thinking about all we've been prepared to do, just to get through this Program. Besides, what if the prize isn't all it's cracked up to be?"

"You think it would be worth the risk of giving up and facing the consequences? After what you've seen? You wouldn't be worried every time you ate meat again for the rest of your life that they might have slipped a bit of human in there for you to chew on? You wouldn't be concerned that armed intruders weren't going to burst into your home one random evening and annihilate your family just to teach you some kind of sick lesson?"

She sighs. "I guess you're right. We need to keep going. We need to see this through. It's lose-lose, but if we make it through the Program, we'll at least have something to show for it. Whether it's worth it, I don't know."

"Yeah, for all we know this whole process will drive us insane and we'll end up locked up as roomies in an insane asylum."

"At least they'd keep us drugged up so we wouldn't keep reliving what's happening to us."

"Wow, we're setting the benchmark really low here. Where our preference is to be coma'd out on pharmaceuticals and wrapped in straitjackets rather than thinking about what our lives have become."

"It's not like we have much of a choice."

We lie there in compatible silence until I finally drift off to sleep. This time, my mind is a void. No dreams, no nightmares. Just deep slumber, which my body and mind so desperately need. I'm so glad Whitney is here as my roommate. I don't think I'd have made it this far through without her.

I laugh out loud when I realize I once worried Gerald smoked a cigarette when he told me he quit for me, when I just ate human flesh. Ah, those were the days of dick people problems. For fuck's sake.

He'd arrived back at the apartment reeking of cigarettes and said, 'Sorry babe, my friend was having a cigarette and I couldn't resist joining him.'

Imagine me coming home now and saying 'sorry honey, I told you I wouldn't eat humans, but I just saw an irresistible deltoid.'

Oh my god, I am mansplaining his cigarette smoking with cannibalism. This Program is really giving me perspective. A warped perspective.

Wow, I guess Donovan is right.

I really can justify just about anything.

CHAPTER TWENTY-ONE

Ruby

"For your final task, you're going to decide who you get to save. Your cohort partner, or yourself. Now that we're down to the final few, the stakes will be even higher. The consequences will be life or death."

Whitney and I lock eyes, and I feel mine widening.

I'm paired with Ryan, and I walk over to him. He places a hand on my own trembling arm and it's reassuring. But what did Carlton just say? One of us has to kill the other? Holy shit. Are these guys fucking kidding? Although after what I've seen, nothing they could challenge us with would be too grotesque. They're fucking sick. I just figured they wouldn't stoop to murder in this creepy old manor. But they already have, so of course they're prepared to do it again. This group of evil people enjoys creating a real-life house of horrors. They prey on our fear. They control us.

I should have listened to Donovan.

There's no getting out of this.

The fire starts in one corner of the room, and for a moment Ryan looks like he's about to bolt. But then I realize the fear in his eyes isn't for himself. He is scared for my life.

He could run and save his own life, or he could stay and attempt to rescue me.

He cries out in agony as the flames jump to his suit jacket, but he doesn't stop trying to release me from the knots that are holding me captive to this blaze. He rips himself free from his jacket, but that only exposes his arms, unprotected against the flames.

The gnarly, acrid smell of burnt flesh enters my nostrils.

Just as he pulls me free, a burning plank of wood collapses from the ceiling.

"Ryan, no!" I scream as it lands right on top of him, smashing him directly in the forehead. He crumples to the ground and I stare helplessly for a moment as I regain circulation in my hands and feet.

"Help!" I cry out, but it's quickly apparent that nobody is coming to rescue us.

I wrap my hands with the remains of his suit jacket and manage to lift the beam, hefting one end of it. I'm grateful that I committed to strength workouts every morning of the past few months, or there's no way I could have dreamed of lifting this away from him. Or maybe it's those superhuman instincts that kick in during an emergency, like when a mother is suddenly able to lift a car off a baby.

I get behind his unconscious form and grab hold of him underneath both arms and drag. He doesn't budge at first, but the floor is thankfully made of polished hardwood and after what seems like a long time but was probably only a second or two, I'm able to start dragging him across the room.

There's a loud groan, and another beam wrenches itself free and tumbles to the floor, landing with a loud boom that shakes the floor beneath us. It's ablaze, and embers fly from it and begin a mesmerizing dance in the breeze, threatening to take up residence in the surrounding dry wood. It's directly in our path, and I need to take a detour, dragging Ryan's frame around the bulky chunk of wood.

Right as we get close to the door, another beam groans above us and dislodges, careening to the floor. I jerk Ryan to the side as the flaming beam falls right in front of us, almost pulling my shoulder out of its socket as we barely avoid the giant piece of wood from landing directly on us. I summon my remaining strength and pull him around this beam, right before the floor behind us collapses to the dark nothingness below.

I glance toward freedom, but there's no way I can pull Ryan's giant frame out of this building.

"Ryan!" I slap him and shake his shoulder. "Ryan! Please wake up! We have to go now!" Ryan shifts, his head moving slightly.

"Ryan! Get up!"

He slowly opens his eyes and glances around, the fire dancing in his pupils. His mouth gapes open as he realizes our situation.

"Please! Stand up!" I yank him underneath his arms and he shakes himself free and gets uneasily to his feet.

"I've got this," he says weakly.

I grab his hand and pull him in the direction of the front door. His stance becomes less clunky as he fully regains consciousness as well as his balance. Suddenly, he's in front of me and pulling me behind him, down the stairs, through the front door and out into the cold, dark night.

We run as fast and as far away from the building as we can.

From outside the gates, we hear an earth-shattering boom. I flinch and Ryan pulls me behind him as the entire mansion goes up in a ball of flames. I tuck into his chest as the wave of heat surges past us.

We turn and look at the remnants of the building that continue to burn wildly, black smoke swirling high into the air. Sirens begin to head in our direction.

"Let's get out of here," I say, and Ryan nods.

"Let me take you home," he says, his arm wrapped firmly around me as if he never wants to let go.

"I think we need to get you to the hospital, actually," I say. I can feel his grip growing weaker, even though he's trying to be strong for me. Sure enough, a moment later he crumples to the ground.

Monitors beep and nurses bustle in and out of the room checking vital signs and administering drips as I sit on Ryan's bed holding his hand.

He smiles weakly at me. "Do you believe me now?"

"Believe what?"

"How much I've grown to care about you?"

"Well, you could have run away and taken the winnings without having to share them with me. Put yourself before me. But instead, you've proven you're a real hero. My hero."

"I'm glad you can see that. I really do think I'm falling in love with you, Ruby Hart."

"Did you just say the 'L' word, Ryan?"

"I believe I did. Although it might be all the drugs."

I playfully punch him in the shoulder and he winces. "Oh my god, sorry! I forgot already!"

He shakes his head and smirks. "It's okay. I'm sure I can find a way for you to repay me."

"Oh you can, can you?"

His eyes twinkle and he wiggles his eyebrows. "Oh yes. I can think of several ways and I plan on making you follow through on every one of them."

"I can't wait." I smile at him and gently caress the line of his stubbled jaw.

Chapter Twenty-Two

R uby

To my surprise, even though the Program isn't officially done, they've let us out to return home before returning for the final elements.

Yes, the Program is still going. Setting fire to part of the manor was apparently always part of the plan, and they have permits ready to begin rebuilding immediately. These people have no limits.

We're allowed to interact with friends, family, the general public. But the one rule is that we're not able to discuss the Program in any way. Doing so is instant grounds for dismissal and the inevitable *consequences* that are always being threatened like an inevitable albatross around our necks.

I'm excited to go home. But I know the Program is still an open chapter in my life, and I won't be getting closure anytime soon.

The apartment looks exactly as it did when I left. My cat is still staying at a friend's place, so it's just me and the empty space. Able to use my phone again, I see a ton of missed calls and texts from Gerald begging to take me back, which I happily ignore.

As a first priority, I call Natasha.

"Hey!" She exclaims excitedly from the other end of the phone. "I'm so excited to hear your voice! I've missed you!"

"Hey, I'm out on parole from my executive leadership course!" That's the code speak we were encouraged to use for the Program when we have to explain our whereabouts without giving anything away. They even provided us with some bullet points on a bogus course where we hone our strategic leadership and decision-making skills to develop high-performing teams or some corporate drivel like that. "Wanna hang?"

"Sure! Mind if I bring Danny?"

"Danny, as in—?"

"Yes! The cute bartender guy! We've become a thing now... I guess you could say things are getting kind of serious! We're talking about moving in together."

"Oh my goodness! I'm so happy for you!" I really am. This is unexpected but my friend truly deserves to find someone who treats her well.

We set up a time to meet and I end the call.

Chapter Twenty-Three

R *uby*

"What do you want? I thought you were never talking to me again." I roll my eyes. "I thought our friendship was done."

"No need to be like that, Ruby," Donovan says, and I immediately notice that something seems off. He's always intense with a tendency to focus on the negative. But this time he has an extra intensity about him, a darkness that passes over his face and makes his eyes burn like dark coals with flecks of gold in them. He's fired up, and I can't imagine what's set him off like this that has anything to do with me.

"The guy that I've been hunting with my team.. well, I have to tell you because it's about to break. I don't want you to hear about it for the first time on the TV."

A nervous lump feels like it's erupting in my stomach. My skin is crawling in anticipation of the news I'm about to hear. I'm not sure what it's going to be, but I know for sure that I one hundred percent won't like it. Every nerve ending in my body is ablaze in fear that my life is about to be irreparably changed.

"It's your father, Ruby. I'm so sorry to have to tell you this. But your father is the person who has been hurting all these women and children over town."

I feel the blood drain from my face and limbs and, as if anticipating my reaction, Donovan reaches out to grab me and stop me from falling.

"I'm so sorry, I should have suggested we sit down first. Come over here and take a seat."

He hurries over to the nearby kitchen counter and pours me a glass of cold water straight from the sink and brings it over to me. "Here, sorry it's not filtered or anything."

Whether the water is filtered or not is the last thing on my mind. I gulp it down hungrily, my mouth suddenly parched as if I just drank a shitload of red wine or maybe some green tea. One of those drinks that suck every last ounce of moisture out of your mouth. Fuck, I wish I had many bottles of red wine right now, even though I don't even like the stuff.

I want to be numb. To not feel. To forget what I just heard.

My father is a rapist. A killer. A pedophile. I feel the contents of my stomach threatening to expel themselves. I shouldn't have drank the water so fast.

"Are you sure?" I whisper, feeling my body start to tremble.

"I wouldn't have shared this with you unless I was one hundred percent sure," he says softly, concern in his eyes. "I'm so sorry. We have some video evidence from a secret entryway into his home, as well as a pretty horrific audit history on his personal computer that our IT forensics department was able to extract. I'll spare you the details. They're pretty gruesome."

Suddenly, all the nights he was away flash into my mind. The business trips where he would spend entire weeks away but wouldn't seem to be able to bring back any stories to share. The nights I would stay up with my mother while she cried, wondering where he was. Presuming he was having an affair or something. God, if she was still alive I bet that she would wish that's 'all' he was doing.

No wonder I'm so fucked up.

With genes like these, I'm doomed.

CHAPTER TWENTY-FOUR

R^{*yan*}

I'm doing everything I can to get my mind off the Program. The flashbacks from the fire have me shrieking with night terrors. Despite my intention to see if there could be something with Ruby, each time I picked up the phone to call or text her I just couldn't follow through. She was a constant reminder of me losing my finger, and of the scars from the fire. It was just too painful. Much easier to lose myself in the vacant life that existed before I even heard of the life-destroying Program.

So I'm at home, indulging myself the way I always used to do when I needed to feel better.

The petite blonde woman takes my cock into her mouth and I groan as she sucks on my tip. I'm rock hard, my gaze fixated as her plump lips wrap around my shaft and she bobs her head up and down my length.

I'll give it to her, Becky is great at blowjobs. Not necessarily the most fun to be around, she can barely hold a conversation. But the way she sucks dick keeps my rapt attention. And she doesn't get offended when I've had enough and send her on her way.

"You like that, baby?" she removes her mouth from my cock to ask me in her nasal voice.

I push her head down. "Get back there and suck my cock," I growl, wanting to focus her on the one thing I invited her over here for.

I know, I'm an asshole. But I don't want to hear her high-pitched voice, let alone engage in conversation with her. I just want to feel her tongue expertly lapping at my head, to feel her sucking my shaft into her mouth, to feel her cupping my balls while she services me. And I want my cum to squirt down her stupid fucking throat. Then I want her to get the fuck out so I can sleep.

Jesus, if I'm not careful she's going to want to stay the night. I just know it. I'll find an excuse why she can't... I'll blame work or something, say I have an early meeting.

I only want her for one thing, even though I'm pretty sure she wants more. I always say I'll never see her again, that she's far too annoying. But sometimes, late at night, she'll call and I'll remember how good she is at this, and I'll let her come over. Shame on me, in some regards. But hey, this dick isn't going to suck itself.

But tonight is different. As good as this feels, I can't get my mind off one thing. One person. It's distracting me from enjoying this as much as I usually do.

Usually I'm pretty good at shoving thoughts out of my mind and just focus on getting off. But I'm struggling not to think about *her*.

Ruby.

Because even though someone else has my cock in their mouth, the only person I can think about is Ruby.

I wish it was her mouth that my cock was sliding into. I wish it was her pillowy soft lips wrapped around my shaft, and her tongue swirling across my tip.

I can't get her out of my mind.

I want her to be here. I want her to stay the night. I want to have a conversation with her.

Who am I becoming?

What is she doing to me, when she's not even here?

I wonder if she's thinking about me. I wonder if she's getting pounded by some random dude. The thought of it is keeping my cock hard, thinking about her getting fucked by someone else. I want it to be me slamming into her pussy while she looks up at me with her gorgeous big eyes.

"Becky?" I mumble, her lips still impaled on my cock.

"Yes babe?" she looks up at me expectantly. What does she think I'm going to do, propose?

"I'm sorry but you've got to go, right away."

"But I—."

"This isn't working for me anymore. I need you to leave."

She huffs and pushes herself up on the bed. "Fuck you," she pouts. "Are you fucking serious?"

"Calm down, get your things and go."

I pull the sheet over my half-firm cock. She huffs and puffs some more while she hastily pulls on her clothes. "You're really something, Ryan," she whines in her nasal voice. "After everything I do for you."

"Don't make yourself look pitiful," I say, just wanting her to be gone, not caring if I come across as callous or cold. "Please just do yourself a favor and leave."

"There's someone else, isn't there?" she says as she looks back one more time on her way out the door.

"Yes, there is going to be someone else."

She gasps, grabs her purse and runs down the hallway. I hear the front door slam behind her.

Sometimes you have to be cruel to be kind.

Chapter Twenty-Five

I try to resist the overwhelming urge to watch the news. I never normally watch media coverage of current events because it's so depressing, but today I feel compelled. Because of, and despite, what I know the headline story is going to be.

I click on the TV and sure enough, the news anchor is speaking in clipped nasal tones about my shitty monster of a father. A banner screams at me from the top of the screen: *Serial Murderer and Rapist Arrested on Multiple Charges.*

A news anchor wearing a dark grey suit and navy blue tie appears on the screen.

"Theodore Wayne Hart was arraigned today on charges including homicide and multiple sexual assaults on women and minors in the local county area. Given the severity of the allegations against him, reliable informants say he's unlikely to be let out on bail. Clearly, the community is strongly advocating that he remain in a maximum security facility pending the outcome of his trial, although he does have a scant few supporters advocating for charges to be dropped."

There's always someone willing to back a loser. It makes me sick, though. How could anyone defend his actions?

As I reflect on my father's horrific transgressions, I worry. I know that I'm not him, but what if there's a part of me in my core that's destined to be just like him? What if nature does really triumph over nurture and conscience and morality, and at the end of the day we're just made of the same fabric our cloth was cut from? I don't think I have it in me to murder or rape, and I know I'd never harm a child. But what if there's something deep inside of me that *is* capable of real darkness?

I guess the Program is proof of my ability to cross over into a world of questionable morality. To make hard decisions for what seems to be the greater good. Or let's be real. My own self-benefit.

Maybe it just takes the right environment, the right triggers, and I'd be capable of anything.

Because of me, people have been injured.

I ate human flesh, for fuck's sake.

Maybe I'm not so different from my father after all.

And maybe that's my destiny.

Chapter Twenty-Six

*R**uby***

"I don't deserve you. I'm unworthy of love. I'm the product of hate, of evil. You don't want to be around that. I feel like I'm contagious and I'll only ever bring anyone but sickness and pain." I blink back tears, but one betrays me and slides down my cheek. My body begins to shudder.

"That's not fair, Ruby! Where is this all coming from?" Ryan's eyes are full of concern and he wraps an arm around my shoulder.

"I don't want to talk about it. I just need to let you go, and let you get on with your life while I get on with mine. Just like you tried to when the Program allowed us to leave."

"I'm so sorry, Ruby. It was just too painful at first. But then I remembered how you made me feel. I realized I was being weak and selfish and instead of learning lessons and being transformed, I was going back to the stupid empty life I had before. You've changed me more than the Program ever could. I can't think about anyone but you. You're all I want and all I need."

"Oh, please tell me how the most popular guy wants me. Like I'd believe that?"

"Ruby, I mean it! I need you. You're everything to me. I believe we could have an amazing life together."

"I—I can't." Sobs wrack my body for a moment, but then an eerie calm washes over me and I calm myself.

Ryan looks panicked, and he reaches out to cover my hand with his but I wrench my arm away. "Please, Ruby," he pleads. "You're really going to walk away after everything we had?"

"I don't feel like I have a choice!" I yell. "You don't understand. This is the only choice I get if I want to protect you!"

"It's not your decision to make, though. I want to be with you. Surely I get to have a say in that, too."

"There's something you don't know about me. That could ruin your life more than the Program ever did." My voice lowers. I'm so ashamed. So scared to share my secret.

"You can tell me anything, Ruby," he says, his voice soft.

"If you must know, my father is Theodore Hart. Yes, the killer rapist one." My mouth contorts in an uncontrollable scowl as I think of the man who calls himself my father. "You must have heard about what he did all over the news."

He pauses for a moment. "I... I already know that, Ruby. And it doesn't matter to me at all."

I look at him in shock. "Then why haven't you said anything about it? How could you not just go running for the hills? Why do you want to have anything to do with me?"

"I—I didn't want to pry," he shrugs. "You've been through enough. I figured you'd tell me when you were ready." He places his hand on mine and this time I don't pull away.

"So you just skirted around it and failed to mention it to me? You wanted to talk about other things when this is literally the most insane thing in my life right now?"

"Ruby," he says, his shoulders slumping as he lets out a sigh. "The truth is, I've been feeling extremely guilty for ghosting you after we were able to return home. I felt like an utter piece of shit. I can't even imagine how you must be feeling."

His gentle voice juxtaposed with what I just shared is too much. The reminder of him ghosting me is just another layer.

"I can't do this," I cry, yanking my hand free once again.

And this time I run. And I don't look back.

Chapter Twenty-Seven

R*uby*

When I get home, I pick up the phone and try to call Natasha but she doesn't answer. I text Donovan but he doesn't reply. Neither does Whitney.

So I do what I do best, even though it's probably the last thing I should do. I pick up a bottle of tequila and I take shot after shot after shot. And I begin to think.

My heart is screaming.

I felt like for once I could trust someone. And everyone told me I was an idiot for placing any trust in any of the guys I ever have. And here I am. Hanging on a fragment.

Who am I trying to prove myself to? The fucking devil? Because if that's the case, I'm playing right into his hands.

I'm waiting for him to laugh at me. To tell me that everything that has happened in my life is all my fault. Just like the others.

Oh my god. Are all guys like this?

Or am I just so shit the worst ones gravitate towards me?

Because apparently I have a knack for it.

The abusive. The gaslighters. The ones who think I am the problem or at least try to make me feel that way.

The ones who ghost me and then pop back up when they feel like it.

The ones who pretend they don't know my worst secrets.

He probably thinks it's hilarious, and now he wants to comfort me by healing my wounds with Band-Aids. Go fuck yourself, asshole.

CHAPTER TWENTY-EIGHT

R *uby*

The next day

"I feel betrayed." I pick up my champagne flute and take a large swig. "How could he go around knowing all this horrific information about me and then not even mention it? It feels like he knew my deepest, darkest secret and held that over me."

"How did he hold it over you, though?" Natasha's tone is thoughtful as always.

"Just by knowing it. It just feels... wrong that he didn't mention it."

"Okay," she shrugs. "I'm totally playing devil's advocate here, but... what if he was trying to protect you? Trying to be there for you without picking at what really is a very fresh wound for you. Maybe he was trying to give you space."

"He was actively avoiding me when he got out of the Program. Said he couldn't bear being in my presence because it was too raw. That I was a reminder of... everything."

"He shouldn't have done that, but he has at least apologized, right?"

"I suppose." I jut out my bottom lip, fully aware I'm pouting like a child while I imbibe my champagne.

"And, it would have been weird for him not to fix that but then bring up your dad, right? I'm sure that would only have served to upset you, and you might not have been able to reset your relationship."

"Since when were you such a Ryan super fan?" I pout, narrowing my eyes at my supposed friend. It feels like a betrayal that she's supportive of my betrayer. And very unlike her.

"Oh, come on. You know I will always have your back," she says, the beginnings of a smirk making their way across her face. "I'm not trying to make light of the situation, because it's pretty fucking serious. But maybe for once in your life your stubborn-ass brain could give someone the benefit of the doubt."

"This is the time you want me to try not to be stubborn?"

"Yep, no time like the present," she replies.

It does seem uncharacteristic of her to be siding with a guy that I've displayed any interest in. Normally, it feels like she's gunning for them from the outset. I know it's coming from a good place, and she's just incredibly protective of me. But sometimes it feels a little overbearing, having her picking apart everything a guy says and does, or doesn't do, the moment I introduce her or even just mention them sometimes.

"Why this change of heart? You hate every guy I've ever mentioned."

"I haven't hated them... well, most of them. I've just seen through their bullshit and wanted to save you the trouble of wasting your time. Because I know you've deserved better, even when you couldn't see it yourself."

Still very ironic coming from her, when she applies such rose-colored glasses to absolutely every man that enters her life with a cute smile and the tiniest ounce of charisma. But that's always been our dynamic, and we've both always been there to pick up the pieces for each other. I get the feeling that's never going to change, although

I'd certainly love it if at some point there were no longer any pieces necessary to pick up. For either of us. Because it's exhausting and because I really do believe that both of us deserve to find our true loves.

"Listen, if he does anything that slightly resembles hurting you, you know I'll kick his ass immediately. But I just have a feeling about this one. You have to trust your own gut, though." She squeezes my arm, her long nails digging in like usual. I don't know why they comfort me so much, but I know if she ever clipped them short I'd be disappointed.

I take a deep breath and slowly exhale. "Okay. You always give me good advice, even when you don't treat yourself the same way."

"I have no idea what you're talking about," she says, grinning at me. Maybe she's more self-aware than I've ever realized, after all.

Maybe she's right. But maybe she's very wrong, and I'm destined to repeat the same mistakes for the rest of my life.

Chapter Twenty-Nine

Ruby

"How are you feeling about everything?" Donovan looks at me with concern in his eyes, and like usual I know he's anticipating my answer. He's gotten so good at reading people from his job, and this has definitely extended to his closest friends and family, which I guess I count as now.

I shrug, my shoulders slumping in resignation. "I don't know. How are you meant to feel when you find out your father is a psycho who hurts women and children?"

"I didn't ask how you're *meant* to feel. I want to know how you, Ruby, feel. I don't think there's a textbook, cookie-cutter way you're meant to feel when you experience something as traumatic as this. Give yourself a break. How do *you* feel?"

I sigh. "Rotten. Like the core of my being is infested with whatever sickness *he* has. I feel like I'm tainted by darkness."

"You aren't your father, Ruby. Remember that. You're nothing like him. It's like the universe, God, whatever you believe in, took the best parts of him—and I truly don't believe any one person is completely evil—and combined them with your mother. Then maybe added a few extra things to make you. You're the very best of them and more. Don't let their actions or inactions define you. They can never take away from how special you are."

"Well thank you for saying that."

"I'm not just saying it to kiss your ass or cheer you up, Ruby. I truly believe every word of it."

"Why are you being so nice to me, anyway? You don't owe me anything."

"It's not about owing anyone anything, Ruby."

"But we're not even together anymore. We haven't been for many years. But you've still just always been here, been around. I really missed you when you said you couldn't be around me because of the Program. I didn't know myself without having you to lean on. And that's not fair to you. I rely on you so much. But I don't see you in any way other than a friend and I don't want to hurt you because of that."

"I know, and I've thought about that a lot as well. As much as I love you, we're just way better off as friends."

"You've really given this a lot of thought? I mean, I agree with you. I just didn't know it had been on your mind."

"You're always on my mind, Ruby. And I've thought through all the permutations. There's no way I could ever share you. I'm far too jealous for that. But I also know that I'm not enough for you on my own."

It's like a slap to the face that stings very badly. This amazing man that I've apparently made to feel like he's not enough. How dare I? "You're more than enough. It's just…" I look down, reflecting on why things didn't work out between us.

"Okay, so I didn't use the right words. That's kind of my thing and part of the issue." He smiles sadly. "Look, what I meant to say is I'm not what you need. I'm not what you're ultimately looking for. And that's okay. It doesn't mean anything is wrong with either of us. It just is the way it is. So I know our ship has likely sailed, but I don't want to spend my life wondering what if I got that wrong. I spent a lot of time soul searching while you were in the Program, Rubes. And I've come to the conclusion that I need to give you up. To truly set you free. But I'll always, always be here for you when you need me. As a friend. As chosen family."

Chapter Thirty

R^{*uby*}

"So, there's really nothing going on with you two? Romantically, I mean." Ryan quirks his eyebrow at me. Is that a little jealousy I detect? Interesting. I resist the urge to smirk.

"Absolutely not. I mean, Donovan and I did used to be in a relationship, but that was a while ago now. I'm grateful for what our friendship has become. I nearly lost him as a friend, going through the Program. It really hurt him when I went against his advice and signed up anyway. I thought he was never going to talk with me again."

"So, what did I see then?" Ryan had walked into the cafe near the tail-end of my conversation with Donovan. This city is large, but it feels like a small town sometimes.

"We hugged. He was consoling me when I was crying. Over you."

"Why would you be crying over me?"

"I thought I'd lost you. That last task... it was almost too much to bear. I don't know how I had the strength to pull you out of there. I've been having flashbacks and nightmares that you didn't make it out of the building alive. If you hadn't, I'm not quite sure what you would have done. And then when you ghosted me, I was just devastated. I really thought we had a connection... and then you just weren't in my life anymore."

His gaze locks with mine, his beautiful eyes feeling like they're boring into my soul. "You really mean that? You wouldn't have just moved on to someone else?"

"Really? You think you're that irreplaceable? Not to me, you're not. I've learned more about you in the past couple of months, and grown closer to you, than anyone ever in my life. That's not something that I could just throw away. There's no 'moving onto the next one' for me. Why? Am I that disposable to you?"

He suddenly looks shattered. "I can't believe you'd even ask me that."

"I—I'm sorry," I say quickly. "I just... I guess I'm waiting for the next person to hurt me. Waiting for the ax to fall. Waiting for the pain to begin again."

He frowns, his brow deeply furrowed and his eyes gentle. "Well that's not going to happen, Ruby. Not from anything I would do to you. I would never treat you that way."

Chapter Thirty-One

R*uby*

A woman with wavy blonde hair and large blue eyes is clinging to Ryan's arm. I feel a coil of jealousy slithering across my belly and into my chest.

They're both animated, and his eyes are flashing as he tries to pry her arm off him.

Even from here, I can tell she probably speaks with one of those shrill, nasal voices that so many women seem to have picked up from reality TV.

She starts to cry, and her dark eye makeup begins to stream down her face. Whatever's going on, it's quite the dramatic scene, and it reinforces my decision to always buy waterproof mascara. The woman eventually storms off. Ryan notices me in the corner and walks over.

"Oh shit, Ruby. I'm really sorry you had to see that."

"Me too. It looked messy." I quirk an eyebrow at him. "What's the deal?"

"Well, it's dealt with now. I don't think she'll be worrying us anymore."

"Who the fuck is she, anyway? It's pretty clear you've fucked before. And she clearly has a thing for you. Anyone in a two-mile radius could hear what she was yelling at you."

He looks down, his brow furrowed. "She doesn't mean anything to me. I can promise you that."

"What, then?" I have flashbacks of Gerald and Clark and no desire to repeat the dramatic events I went through with them. I'm ready to start sticking up for myself and demanding answers. I deserve that much.

"Okay, I—before I met you, and before we were truly together, I guess I used her for sex. I'm not proud of it. She's a very annoying person. I was lonely, I guess."

I smirk at his brutal truthfulness. "Well, at least you're honest I suppose. What now, then? Are you going to just let her keep popping back into your life?"

"Oh, hell no. She has no place in my life anymore. Consider her blocked in every capacity."

"Do you think she'll survive?"

"Not my concern."

"So, you know some things about me before the Program. Are there any skeletons in your closet that you'd like to share with me, Ruby? Anything you think I might want to know?" He's teasing me again, his eyes twinkling in the soft candlelight in the restaurant he's taken me to for a romantic dinner.

"Well, there was one night, early in the Program...". My voice trails off.

He quirks an eyebrow, clearly interested in what's coming next.

"Yeah... Whitney and I kind of hooked up."

"Wait, what?!" He almost spits out the wine he just sipped from a crystal goblet. If I didn't have his full attention before, I certainly do now. "Tell me more," he says, smirking. "Spill."

I tell him about Whitney's and my passionate encounter, his eyes darkening with lust as he visualizes my words as if it's like a porn film running in his mind. I have no doubt his cock is straining in his pants at the thought of Whitney and I together.

"Oh, to have been a fly on that wall," he says, wiggling his eyebrows at me.

I roll my eyes in response, but then I grin.

"Look, it didn't mean anything. Emotions were heightened, and everyone was a bit giddy. We were clinging to each other literally, because we were all failing to cling to our sanity."

"Are you sure that's all it was?" He looks skeptical, his brow quirking skyward. "You're not going to leave me and run off with your old roommate?"

I nod without hesitation. "It was nothing more than that. But I also have no regrets."

Out of the corner of my eye, I notice the blonde girl has entered the restaurant—Becky I think Ryan said her name was—and is standing off in the corner, watching us.

"Oh god, she's here. The one that was screaming at you. She's full-on stalking us, standing in a restaurant watching us eat. I thought you said she was gone for good."

"Are you fucking kidding me? I really thought I could get her to leave this time. I thought my words had sunk in loud and clear." His eyes are dark with rage and he turns to openly glare at her.

I lean forward and place a hand on his arm. "Look, I can think of a way to get rid of her once and for all that won't get either of us arrested."

"Oh yeah?" He raises an eyebrow. "Are you thinking what I'm thinking?"

"That this calls for a toast? And to show her that you really are otherwise occupied?" I raise my glass.

He nods and also raises his glass. "Precisely."

"To being an asshole and delivering a message successfully."

"To being an asshole and delivering the clearest message possible, by showing her what true love looks like."

We clink glasses, and lean in for a kiss. I don't mind putting on a show. Especially when his lips feel so good against my own, and his tongue teases mine. What started as a tentative kiss turns into a full-on make-out session, our clothes only remaining on due to the barrier of the table that sits between us.

I open one eye and try not to laugh as I see her turn on her heel and run off in the other direction. "I think she got the message," I say.

"About fucking time," he replies, kissing me again.

I don't like that he used her. But he at least admits it.

And if the Program has taught me anything, it's that I used to spend way too much time worrying about being a good person.

Now's my time to focus on living. On enjoying life.

Chapter Thirty-Two

R *uby*

"So who was she?! Do we need to cut her?" Natasha is enthralled as I recount what happened at dinner with Ryan.

"Thankfully, no," I laugh, "although I was tempted."

"It reminds me of the first day we went and hung out at the club while Danny was working, and I saw him with those women. My stomach was burning, and I couldn't stop clenching my jaw when I saw him speaking to them like that. My heart was racing. It was awful, and all I wanted to do was throw up. But something in me told me that he was just doing his job, and to give him a chance. To cut through all my doubts and trust him. I felt like an idiot, and like I was setting myself up for heartbreak, but I'm so glad I did."

"I feel that on such a deep level," I say, and I truly do. I'm still working my way through the same physical reactions, and I know I'll need to get over them and learn to trust Ryan if we have any chance at being a strong couple. But I also know my past experiences are going to keep me alert for any flags. I might have been born naïve, but now I'm far from that.

"So things are going well with you and Danny, I take it?"

Natasha beams, and she suddenly looks a little shy which is very unusual for her. "Well... things are going very well, you could say. In fact...". She lifts up her left hand and wiggles her fingers. I immediately notice she's sporting a sparkly ring, but it's on her middle finger. "Don't freak out, we're not engaged. It's a promise ring. And he got it for this finger so if I'm ever sitting at his bar and think he's getting too flirty with one of his patrons I can just flip him the bird. I've already used it once or twice and he's received the message loud and clear." She giggles, and I can't help but laugh either. This woman never ceases to amaze me.

"Well, I'm so happy for you," I smile.

"And you? Any cute guys in your Program?"

"Oh, you could definitely say that. But I need to keep things quiet for now. I promise as soon as I'm able to share more, I will." I can't wait to tell her all about Ryan, and to introduce them to each other, but clearly that's going to have to wait until the Program has been signed off as done and dusted, as Carlton would say.

I shiver as I recall the slender man with his chiclet teeth.

If I never see that man smile his creepy, thin-lipped smile again it would be too soon.

But if he wants to meet me to announce I've graduated from the Program, I'm sure I would quickly change my mind.

But before I worry about that, there's someone I need to see.

Chapter Thirty-Three

R *uby*

"How could you do this? To your victims? To mom? To me?" Blood thuds through my temples and I don't even try to keep my voice down.

"You think you're so perfect," my father scoffs. "Always running around thinking you're better than everyone else." His body looks frail, like he's aged in triple time since the last time we spoke. Maybe it's karma that has wrinkled his features, receding his hairline and making him look like a pale, sad old man in his bright orange jumpsuit. Age spots cover his face, and hi mouth is down-turned in a perpetual scowl.

"Why would you hurt those people?" I feel my whole body shake, and I can't stop yelling. "You're a fucking monster!"

"Don't you think it might be because it happened to me? That maybe I learned it from somewhere?"

"Oh, you were attacked were you? That sounds like a really convenient excuse."

"You're a real piece of work, you know that?" He growls, his jagged yellow teeth bared. "Your mother should have had an abortion. I told her to, but she refused to listen. I even tried punching her in the stomach and pushing her down the stairs, but you've always been a resilient little bitch, even in the womb. I couldn't get rid of you no matter how hard I tried."

"Well, at least you never touched me, you sick fuck."

"Couldn't bring myself to. You're the last person I would ever want to touch," he growls and spits on the floor, leaving a blob of saliva that I can't stop looking at.

"You're incapable of love. You're full of hate."

"You could say that. Although I did care about you and your mother, for a time at least."

"You couldn't have. Otherwise you never would have done the things you did. You would have found a way to control yourself. Instead of ruining my mother's life the way you did. And now you're trying to ruin mine. Who would want to have anything to do with someone who came from you?"

"Oh, stop with your holier than thou bullshit, Ruby. I'm sick of hearing it. I don't know why you even bothered to come and visit if all you're going to do is attack me. But you always have been a fucking bitch. And besides, the apple didn't fall all that far from the tree, did it? Be honest with yourself. You're just as fucked up as I am, maybe more. I know some of the stuff you've done and it's pretty messed up. You've caused a lot of grief for a lot of people. That's why I never touched you. You make my skin crawl."

Blood is thumping so hard in my temples and chest that I feel like I'm about to pass out, and my gut is churning like an acidic ocean in a storm.

"Honestly, I wish they had the death penalty here for someone like you. I hope you rot away here, and that nobody ever comes to visit you. You deserve to die alone and unhappy. You deserve for others to do to you what you did to those poor people."

I blink back tears as pictures of his victims start to flash back in my mind. As much as I tried to stay away from the media coverage, I've pored over picture after picture of women and young children, some of whose lives he took. Others kept their lives but lost their innocence. So many of them.

I feel guilt and shame for what he did, and for being linked with him.

"Guard!" He screams for assistance from one of the corrections officers waiting on his side of the partition. "Get me out of here, now! I can't stand this little bitch."

The guard approaches and unshackles him from the cold metal desk.

My father looks back one last time, and I see the pure hatred in his eyes.

Normally, an icy gaze like that would cause me to shiver or to be afraid. But right now, I only feel numb.

This wasn't the closure I hoped for, but this man always had a pattern of letting me down.

At least I know I won't have to go through this pain again, because I'm deeply aware within my soul that this was the last time I'll ever have to see him.

And good riddance.

He can burn in hell as far as I'm concerned.

Chapter Thirty-Four

Ruby

"I think I've proven to you that I'm strong. Not broken, like you thought at first."

"Oh, Ruby, I never thought you were broken. I thought you were downright gorgeous right from the moment I first laid eyes on you. Intriguing, different, special. And clearly you're very strong."

Our mouths connect in a passionate kiss, our tongues hungrily exploring each other.

We briefly part while I pull his shirt from his body, revealing his rippling six-pack and rock-hard pecs, highlighted by his golden tan. Running my gaze and hands over him I can barely stop myself from drooling. This man is a real-life god.

"Oh, Ryan," I murmur as he rips off my shirt and expertly unhooks my bra before cupping my breasts in his massive palms.

We could have picked a sexier location than my cluttered, run-down apartment, but he doesn't seem to mind and any semblance of self-consciousness dissipates as I see the way he devours me with his eyes and gently squeezes a nipple in each hand..

"God, Ruby. You're so beautiful," he murmurs, pressing his body against mine so that I feel his hardness through his pants and my own. I wrap my arms around his neck again and our lips and tongues once again connect. His lips are soft and plump, and the way his tongue caresses mine only adds to my arousal. I could kiss this gorgeous man for the rest of our lives and could never get enough. I'd follow him into the afterlife just so I could keep feeling his lips on mine.

I reach one hand down and rub it against his hardness. "Oh, Ruby," he groans, and I smile up at him with hooded, lust-drunk eyes. I'm so happy in this moment I can almost feel them twinkling.

Everything we've been through together flashes through my mind. For a moment I flash back to the fire and hearing his terror-filled screams as the flames seared his flesh. I push the memory out of my head for now, refusing to let anything mar this precious moment where we can finally be together on our terms.

I unzip his jeans, pulling them down quickly followed by his boxer briefs. "Oh baby," he groans again as I begin to stroke his massive cock.

"You didn't tell me everything about you was huge," I grin up at him, causing him to smirk.

"I wanted to find out on your own time, but only if you were a good girl," he grins back at me, his eyes darkening with lust. "And you have been a very good girl, Ruby."

His husky voice makes me melt further, and I almost fall to the ground when he gently scoops me up and places me on the rectangular table at the side of the room. He dips his head and gently sucks on my nipple and I moan as an electric shock of pleasure jolts from his tongue straight to my core.

He gently removes my pants, and I gasp as he reaches down and brushes his hand against my pussy, dipping a finger into my wetness and trailing it up to my clit.

He kneels down in front of me, and I cry out with pleasure as he dips his head forward and begins to lap at my clit. He flattens his tongue and I moan as he inserts two fingers back into my soaked pussy and thrusts them in and out while he feasts on me. It's like he knows exactly where and how to touch me without me needing to say a single word. Angling his tongue in just the right places. Without warning, he sinks his tongue deep into my pussy, tongue fucking me, and I gasp as I feel him tasting me. "Fuck, Ruby," he growls. "You're the best thing I've ever tasted."

I buck my hips rhythmically as he returns the attention of his tongue to my clit and slides two fingers back inside me, and then a third. He devours me as if I'm his last meal, and it's not long before I feel the coil deep within me tightening to the point of no return.

"Fuck, Ryan! I'm about to come!"

"Mm, come for me baby girl," he growls, which sets me off as he immediately returns his tongue to working on my clit. My hips buck on their own accord as my body explodes in a wild orgasm that shoots waves of pleasure throughout my body, my head flying back and stars appearing in my peripheral vision. "Holy fuck!" I yell, as he continues to apply pressure to my clit with his tongue, and he keeps working my pussy with his fingers, feeling me clenching tightly around him until my orgasm finally subsides.

"Good girl," he grins up at me from between my thighs, sliding his fingers out of me.

I lean back on my elbows and smile lazily down at him. This feels like a dream I don't want to wake up from. I hope I never do.

"Do you want me to fuck your sweet pussy now, Ruby?" he growls as he stands up, and I can't help but stare directly at his big cock wondering if I'm going to be able to take the whole thing.

"Fuck, yes please," I moan. "If you fit," I wink.

"Oh, I'll make sure I fit," he grins back at me.

I can't wait to feel him inside me, and I don't need to wait long at all.

He slams his giant hard cock into me, and I'm so wet that it glides in to his hilt in one go. I cry out with surprise and pleasure as he grabs me tightly by the hips for leverage and rails the shit out of me. I've never been fucked so hard and fast in my life, and it's the most unreal boundary of pleasure and pain that will have me craving him forever more.

"Oh fuck!" I cry out. I can't think of anything else to say. I'm delirious with pleasure as he continues to sink his cock deep into me, pulling it out almost all the way and then slamming it back in.

Ryan

I flip her over and growl, "Get on your hands and knees," and she eagerly complies. I groan as she rears her hips backwards, giving me a full display of her glistening pussy and her ass. Using one fist, I grab hold of her hair and yank her neck back, eliciting a deep moan as I use my other hand to line myself up with her entrance and once again slam myself into her tight pussy. "Oh my fucking god!" she screams, as I once again begin to plow her. I wouldn't normally go this hard but I've never felt anything this good and I can't help myself, It's like I've lost all control as I continue to thrust my cock in and out of her tight cunt. "Fucking hell, Ruby," I growl. "This is the best pussy I've ever had in my entire fucking life." And I'm not blowing smoke up her ass. She has the finest pussy I've ever felt in my life. It's like we fit together perfectly even though I'm physically so much larger than she is.

"I could say the same about your cock," she pants, continuing to cry out with pleasure at each thrust.

"Fuck, Ruby!" I yell as my own orgasm peaks and I release inside of her while her pussy continues to contract around me. I grab her by the hips, slamming myself back into her as far as I can go while she milks me of every last drop.

Chapter Thirty-Five

Ruby

"You're... you're leaving?"

I get a weird feeling in the pit of my stomach, like a stone has been dropped.

"Yeah. The Program was... a lot. As you know, more than most people. It's time for me to do something different. To give back."

"So what are you going to do, Whitney?"

"I know it's super cliche but....".

"Oh my god. You're joining the fucking Peace Corps."

She blushes. "Don't laugh at me!"

"Ahaha! You are! But I'm only teasing because of the ads. They're everywhere right now!"

"Yeah. They worked on me. I was watching an episode of reality TV and they kept coming on. And watching rich women yell at each other suddenly wasn't enough for me anymore."

"Well, before you go... there's one thing I need to ask of you. A favor. One I think you might be okay with...".

Chapter Thirty-Six

*R**uby*

"Babe... I could tell you were a bit jealous of what I had with Whitney. And how you had some questions about what it was like. With her, I mean?"

"Yeah... that was a while ago." Ryan shrugs, half-listening and I ogle his big, broad shoulders. I can't get enough of this man. "I think I'm over it. Mostly."

"Well... I have a surprise for you." I grin at him.

He quirks his eyebrow. "What do you mean?"

"Well..." I walk up to him and gently massage both of his shoulders. "I want to show you what it was like."

"What?" Now I have his rapt attention. "You have video footage? Rad."

"No, silly."

As if on cue, there's a knock at the front door.

I guide their faces together and they kiss. My pussy clenches as I watch their tongues begin to explore each other. Unreal. Two of my favorite people making out in front of me. Under my guidance. And I'm about to watch them both. Have them both.

I guide Whitney's face toward mine, and can see Ryan's cock straining against his pants as I begin to undress her. I unbutton her shirt, removing it to reveal a sexy red lace bra. I pull the cup down from one of her perky breasts and suck her nipple into my mouth. Ryan groans as he watches me twirl my tongue around her pebbled bud. I unhook her bra completely and motion for Ryan to join me. He eagerly complies, bending his head to take her other breast into his mouth, twirling his tongue around her nipple. My pussy twinges and I can feel my own arousal as I watch him sucking on her breast.

I unbutton and lower her shorts, and Ryan watches eagerly as I remove her lace panties and guide her over to the couch and get her to sit down facing us.

I spread her thighs wide apart, the way I've come to know she likes. It exposes her glistening pussy, and I lower my head to her pink wetness.

He leans over my shoulder and I feel his warm breath on my neck as I explore her with my mouth. I enjoy the sensation of her sweet taste and her smooth walls on my tongue.

"Baby, you should taste her too."

"Are you sure?"

"Of course. You'd be missing out if you didn't."

He dips his head down and a jolt of pleasure rushes through me as I watch him begin to lap at her pussy with his expert tongue. She moans at his touch.

We both take turns, licking and sucking on her clit and sliding our fingers deep into her pussy while she moans in pleasure. Together, we guide her to an orgasm that causes her to cry out and buck and writhe in pleasure as the waves of pleasure crash over her. Ryan and I turn to each other, kissing each other passionately, our tongues wrestling and swapping her arousal between us.

We move to the bedroom where Whitney lays down on her back, her pussy glistening in the soft light of the overhead lamp. I guide Ryan over to Whitney and watch as he climbs on top of her and places his hands on her curvy hips. His cock is rock hard, and I help guide him into her soft, pink wet entrance. He groans as he glides into her and she lets out a small cry as his girth stretches her walls.

"Oh my fucking god, Ruby! You were right!"

I place my hand on his back to reassure him I'm totally okay with this, and he begins to slide slowly in and out of her. I enjoy the sight of his large dick emerging and then plowing back into her glistening pussy, the sound of her wetness audible in the large room.

Fuck, this is so hot. I should have made this happen earlier. But then again, I probably needed this amount of time to be okay with it. To encourage it to happen.

"Get over here," she growls, and I know exactly what she means.

I move to her front and lay down in front of her, facing upwards.

She dips her head down and begins to feast on me. I look up and make eye contact with Ryan as he continues to ram his hard cock deep inside her while she laps at my pussy.

She slowly kisses her way down my body, stopping at my breasts. Trailing her lips across one of my nipples, she takes one into her mouth and bites down, gently at first and then more firmly. I yelp at the feeling of her sharp teeth, but pain is mixed with pleasure, and I moan as ripples shoot from my nipple down to my core. My pussy twinges, and I can feel arousal beginning to work its way out of me.

Her head continues to descend further down my body, and she stops to trace her tongue around my belly button, then showering it with soft kisses. I moan as she pulls my thighs apart and hungrily eyes my pussy, slick with wetness and anticipation of what's about to happen.

"God, you're perfect," she growls, and dips her head between my thighs. I moan with pleasure as I feel her tongue trace its way across my slick folds, landing on my clit. She sucks my swollen clit into her mouth and I cry out as she applies a little pressure with her teeth. She lowers her head further and I moan as she inserts her tongue into my entrance, tasting me, devouring every drop of my arousal.

She returns her attention to my clit, flattening her tongue against it and then devouring me as she plunges three of her fingers into my entrance. I moan as she thrusts them in and out, the sound of my wetness audible in the room.

The coil within me tightens and I feel myself getting closer and closer until I can't take it anymore. Pleasure courses through me with such ferocity I feel like I'm about to explode, white spots exploding in my periphery as I arch my back and writhe forcefully against her tongue. Her fingers continue to work my pussy as my hips buck and I ride out my orgasm.

It doesn't take long for my orgasm to build, the coil wrapping tighter and tighter within me. Ryan is amazing at eating pussy, but Whitney is even better. A woman's touch, maybe. Either way, I'm not complaining.

Her head mashes further into me each time he thrusts, and it adds an extra dimension as her tongue works its magic on my clit. "Jesus, fuck. You two," I cry out. It's so incredibly hot, watching his hips thrust as his cock smashes into her pussy from behind, her gorgeous ass high up in the air.

I don't feel a hint of jealousy. We all know what we're doing. That this is a one and done. And we've all come through this incredibly traumatic experience and now we're replacing it with... with this. With a shared memory that doesn't involve death or gore. Just bodies. Naked ones. And a hell of a lot of pleasure.

Ryan looks at me, his eyes dark with lust.

"Get over here," he growls. "I want to come inside you while she watches, Ruby."

He rams his cock into me and I'm so wet he slides in easily despite his sizable girth. I cry out regardless, because he feels amazing. Whitney watches as he begins to pound me with a ferocity I haven't experienced before, even though he's given it to me very hard on multiple occasions. I moan each time he thrusts into me.

Glancing over, I see Whitney touching herself as she watches his cock sliding in and out of me.

I feel his body tense and he lets out a groan as he empties himself into me.

We lie together, sated, limbs tangled, before Whitney gets up and puts her clothes back on.

"Still getting your ticket to Botswana?" I grin at her.

"I'm having second thoughts after that," she laughs and winks at me. "But yes, I still need to go."

"You're always welcome back," I smile at her, swiping a tendril of her hair behind her ear. "I'm so proud of you for doing this, though. I think you'll get a lot out of it."

"Me too." She smiles back and leans forward to give me a tender kiss.

"I've never met someone like you, and I know I never will again. And that's okay." She presses her lips together. "Our time together is something I'll always remember. You're very special, Ruby. I hope you realize that."

I smirk. "Oh, I know."

She also smirks and taps me on the shoulder as if to tell me off for my new overconfidence.

"Good luck out there. Send me a postcard."

"Girl, it's 2023. You know I'll email you. Or text." We both laugh.

I watch as she heads out the door. She looks over her shoulder with a smile, and blows me a kiss.

"You're very special too, Whitney," I whisper to myself. I wonder if I'll ever see her again, but also weirdly I know I'll be okay if I don't. I think our chapter is closed, after all. Ryan really is all that I need.

But it sure was fun having Whitney around, too.

Chapter Thirty-Seven

Ruby

"Thank you for sharing her with me. I never expected that," Ryan smiles at me, adoration twinkling in his eyes.

"I just know you needed to experience it for yourself," I shrug and smile back. "To see that we just... work, somehow. But also that you don't need to be jealous."

"Well... I'm going to remember that night forever." He grins and wiggles his eyebrows. "It's staying in my spank bank. Let me put it that way."

I laugh. "Good. You deserve all the best memories to erase the other ones."

"You know, Ruby. You really are all that I need. And all that I want. I couldn't and wouldn't want to imagine life without you."

"I feel the same way, babe. I'm so lucky to have you in my life."

"Are you sorry about the way we met? Do you have any regrets?"

"Regrets aren't healthy. I mean, reflections are. Like thinking about what you might have done differently given the chance. If it helps to set you up to think about what you might do in the future. But trying to reset the past is never going to actually change anything, no matter how hard you try. Right?"

"I totally agree. And I don't regret anything that led me to meeting you."

Chapter Thirty-Eight

R^{uby}

"Congratulations on completing the program, Ruby. As you know, not everybody made it through." Carlton's lips purse and I do my best not to shiver at the sight. "But before we give you your prize, there's one final stipulation. In order to be eligible, you need to nominate one person in your life to be part of the next cohort. This is mandatory, and without doing so you forfeit your right to a changed life. The program board also has a right to implement mandatory consequences the way it did for people who dropped out of the program or who were otherwise eliminated."

"What the fuck? This isn't fair!" This Program is the gift that keeps on giving, it seems.

"You may review the waiver you signed at the outset of the program. You'll see that you clearly signed up for this rule. Paragraph 35(j) for reference."

"Wait, but I—." I grab the slightly crumpled paper out of my bag, and review my copy of the program's lengthy waiver.

Very clearly, it says what Carlton pointed out. Oh my god, I've always been terrible at reading terms and conditions when it comes to contracts, and now it's really come back to bite me in the ass.

"So *we* were nominated for the Program?"

"You know we don't like it when you ask too many questions. So don't push it, Ruby. But our Program hasn't changed since its inception, so read between the lines."

My mind races. Who would have had the audacity, or worse the hatred, to nominate me? Who could hate me that much that they'd want to put me through this.

I know it wasn't Donovan, given he didn't want me to be in the Program in the first place.

It wasn't Natasha, because she has no idea about what the Program actually entails.

This isn't fair.

Just as well I know just the person I'm going to nominate.

Gerald is about to be offered the opportunity of a lifetime. And his ego is so huge there's no way he's going to be able to pass it up.

Not that I can talk. I signed up, after all. But my reasons were different.

And there's no way in hell that he will be able to make it through.

"I think this is reason to celebrate." He grins at me, his eyes twinkling. I can't believe that both of us made it through, both Ryan and me. Whitney too, although she's already on her flight to join the Peace Corps.

I quirk an eyebrow. "Oh yeah? What do you have in mind?"

"Why don't you let me show you? I think that would be easier than trying to describe it. And definitely more enjoyable."

"Oh, is that an invitation?" I grin at him and wiggle my eyebrows. "Because, if so, I accept. Effective immediately."

He winks, and he looks so sexy I almost melt into a puddle on the floor. "I was going to make you wait."

I pout and look up at him through my eyelashes. "That's not fair. Don't be such a tease. If we've learned anything from the Program, it's that we don't know how long we have. Or what might come down our path."

"So you're saying you think we should seize the day and do it right here, right now?"

I place my hand on his cock which is already beginning to harden through his jeans, and flash him a killer smile. "Yes, that's exactly what I'm saying."

"What my lady wants, my lady gets," he growls.

I turn around and grind against him. He lowers my pants and caresses my cheeks, before I hear the familiar sound of him undoing and lowering his own pants.

I feel the head of his rock-hard cock pressed against the entrance to my ass. He slowly presses himself inside, inch by inch, until he's completely inside me.

He fucks my ass with his big cock, reaching around to caress my pussy.

With his other hand, he spanks me on the ass and I enjoy the pleasant sting as he continues to thrust his cock in and out of me.

"That's for making me wait so long for this," he leans forward and growls in my ear. "Just as well you're being a good girl now."

I shiver at his breath tickling my ear, and his words just about make me melt as I continue to hold my hips steady so he can continue to pump himself into my ass. My whole body breaks out in goosebumps as he thrusts his cock deep into me. I glance over at the mirror and see

Ryan's eyes on mine. They're so sexy, flecked with gold and dark with lust as he watches his cock slide in and out of my ass. "You like this, Ruby?" he growls. "You like it when I fuck you in your gorgeous little ass?"

"Mmhmm," I moan, and I mean it. I would let him do this every day, if only my pussy and my mouth wouldn't feel neglected. I definitely intend on incorporating this into our regular activities. I feel intoxicated by how good his cock feels as he slides in and out of me.

"Oh fuck," he growls. "I'm about to come."

My own pleasure continues building, and I reach down to finger my clit while Ryan continues to grind his hips rhythmically against my ass. He reaches his massive hand around to join mine, running his fingers along my slick pussy and teasing my clit. The coil within me continues to tighten. I'm close as well. "Me too, baby," I rasp.

"You're going to come for me like a good girl?"

"Yes, baby," I moan. A jolt of pleasure rips through my body as I reach my peak, his fingers strumming against my clit as he drives his cock deep into my ass. I feel him still for just a moment and then his hips buck as he pulls me down hard against him with his free hand. He's balls deep within me as he releases his seed deep inside me. I feel my pussy pulsating as my ass milks his cock, and he grunts as he reaches the peak of his orgasm. "Fuck, Ruby," he rasps as he fills me up.

I gasp for breath, and he wraps his arms around me from behind. "God, you're perfect, Ruby," he pants. "So fucking perfect."

Chapter Thirty-Nine

R *uby*

I'm roused from my deep sleep to the pleasant feeling of a tongue lapping against my clit. I moan as a mouth softly blows cool air and then sucks my clit inside, followed by two strong fingers sliding inside of me.

God, I love it when he wakes me up like this. It's the best way to start the day.

I also enjoy just waking up to the feeling of his massive arms wrapped around me, his muscular body the perfect big spoon to my own little spoon. I'd call that a close second. A girl could get used to this. I'm already getting kind of used to it, but I know I won't ever take it for granted.

Returning to the top of the bed, he flips me onto my side with my back facing him, and I moan as he slides his massive cock inside me from behind. This position allows him to glide all the way into me, right to his hilt, while he holds onto my hips for leverage with his powerful hands.

"You like that, baby?" he growls into my ear, and I moan, "Mmh-mm," as he begins to thrust his cock in and out of my now-soaked pussy. After a few more pleasurable thrusts, he whispers that he wants to be on top. He slides out of me and flips me onto my back, and rests on one forearm while he uses his other hand to guide himself to my entrance and slides all the way in again.

I wrap my thighs around his firm torso and gaze up at his strong chest and broad shoulders, and his strong arms that flank my body. He starts slowly, gliding in and out of me. His pace soon quickens, and he rails his rock-hard cock into me, each thrust causing me to cry out with pleasure as his cock slams into my pussy. He props himself up higher on his forearms and begins to pull nearly all the way out and slam himself back in. Looking down, I can see his cock as he pounds it into me, withdrawing it to the tip only to slam it straight back into me again.

He's so fucking hot, I could never tire of this view. Or his cock. It's mine for life. And he feels the same way about me. He's made that clear. Program or not, I'm one lucky girl.

I feel his balls slapping against my pussy as he thrusts in and out of me. "Do you like it when I'm balls deep inside you with my big fat cock?" he growls, lowering himself onto his forearms again so his body presses firmly onto mine while he continues to plow me.

"Mmhmm, I love it, baby," I moan. "Fuck my pussy. You feel so fucking good."

"Oh I'll fuck your pussy alright," he growls. "I'm going to destroy it. I'm going to fuck you so hard you'll feel it for days. You're going to remember who you belong to."

"I'm all yours, baby," I moan. I love it when I can continue to feel him for days after we fuck.

He tilts his pelvis, angling himself so that my clit rubs against him while I grind my hips in rhythm with his. He holds my tips tightly for leverage as he slams himself into me. I know his strong hands will probably leave fingerprints as a pleasant reminder of how firmly he's holding onto me while he pounds himself into me.

Taking control, I flip us over and position myself over his hardness. I slam my wet pussy down on his cock which glistens with my arousal, riding him, enjoying the feeling of having him deep inside me. And of being in control of our pace and our rhythm. He grasps my hips again, this time helping to angle me as I impale myself on his shaft over and over again. Tingles of pleasure radiate through my body, and I focus on the sensation of his large cock dragging against my walls each time it slides in and out of me. I love the feeling of having him as deep inside me as possible. And of sliding almost completely off him before slamming myself back down again so we can both feel his length and his girth traveling all the way back into me.

I buck my hips, angling myself so that my clit rubs against him, and I feel the coil deep within me tightening. "I'm close, baby," I pant as the pleasure quickly mounts. My heart is racing as the sensation continues to build, and I know my orgasm is closing in. "Me too," he rasps, and he bucks beneath me, increasing the rhythm of my pussy ramming onto his cock. I moan and cry out with each thrust as he holds onto me harder and begins to pound himself into me from below. I'm fairly certain he's slamming into my cervix at this point, his cock filling my pussy up each time he's all the way in. The room echoes with the sound of our bodies slapping against each other and my arousal, and the air hangs thick with the scent of sex as he continues to drive me onto his rock-hard cock.

He tweaks my nipples, his fingers tugging at my piercings and causing electric tingles to shoot from my nipples down to my already stimulated core. I buck against him as an orgasm slams through my body, radiating waves of pleasure. Little white sparks burst in my peripheral vision as I tilt my head back, close my eyes and cry out in pleasure.

My pussy convulses around his cock as my orgasm reaches its peak, sending him over his own edge, and I feel him release into me, his cock pulsing as his seed flows into my welcoming body. He groans, his eyes closing for a second as pleasure overtakes his body. I wrap my legs tightly around him, pulling him as deep inside me as he can go while he continues to ride his peak.

Both satisfied, I lean down and wrap my arms around him, kissing him on his neck. He tilts his head up and plants a soft kiss on my lips.

"Mmm, I want you to stay inside me all day," I moan, relaxing into his arms.

"I want to be inside you all day," he whispers back, trailing his hand across my shoulder and down my back. He kisses me, his lips exploring mine. "You really are very special, you know that, Ruby?"

I smile back at him. Here I am with this absolute dreamboat of a man, and he's telling me how special I am.

Suddenly, all the moments that led up to this flash into my mind. But this time, I'm able to push them back just as quickly.

I'm ready to be here, to be present in this moment, with this person who values and respects me. And who gives me the absolute best cock I've ever experienced.

This is our time. And by god I think we've both earned it.

How I wish I knew then what I know now. But the ending wouldn't be the same without having gone through the journey to get to this point. To start life with the same knowledge you end with would be a sad, one-dimensional experience. Without the scars, the bruises and the pain. How could you truly appreciate the outcome if you didn't experience this challenges that built you into who you ultimately become?

Sometimes I wonder how my past self would view me now. Have I become more ruthless? More willing to do anything to get by? I'm sure past me would judge present and future me as depraved, of breaching some moral code to get where I am today. But do I regret anything I did? No. Would I do it again? Hell, yes.

Gerald's funeral was pretty lame. I was one of the few people who attended. It turns out I wasn't the only one who thought he was more than a bit of a jerk. How funny that the brunette whore and her blonde friend from his office didn't show up. Turns out his dick wasn't as good as he thought it was, clearly.

I know, I know, I'm being petty. But he deserves it.

Not that he can hurt me anymore. The Program made sure that he couldn't. I had no doubt he wouldn't make it far through.

Ironically, he forgot to take me off his insurance as his primary beneficiary. I inherited a lot of money from him. His mother tried to contest it, of course, but she had no luck because the Program provided me with the best of lawyers. Even better than hers. Being a graduate of the Program is already proving its value.

Her face when the judge ruled in favor of me was priceless. I wish I'd been able to take a picture. As a gesture of goodwill, I mailed her the overstuffed cushions that I threw at Gerald the day I broke up with him. The remaining ones I didn't shove in his suitcase to take with him when I kicked him out, that is.

They were sent anonymously, but she'll know where they came from.

She might see them as a threat, but I think of them as a reminder to stay away from me.

Sometimes I see them in the shadows. They're always watching, listening. Occasionally there will be tests that require me to reinforce my loyalty to the Program.

But I never waver. I play by the rules.

I have no time for their consequences.

So I'll continue doing what I have to do to keep life this sweet.

And I have no regrets.

Blood and Sand (Dark Reverse Harem Romance)

- Sea of Snakes

- Sea of Sinners

- Sea of Rage

- Sea of Pain

- Sinners, Rage & Pain: The Brixton Trilogy

Billionaire's Takeover Collection

- Irreversible Decision

- Compelling Proposal

- Love Merger

- The Billionaire's Takeover Collection (all 3 of the above!)

Novellas

- Love in a Seedy Motel Room

Join me on social media:

Facebook: @heidistarkauthor

Instagram: @heiditstarkauthor

TikTok: @heidistark_author

Twitter: @heidistarkauthr

Websitehttps://heidistarkauthor.com

Heidi Stark is an indie dark romance author who grew up in New Zealand and now resides in the US.

She is inspired by the locations she visits on her travels, and the people she meets along the way.

When she's not writing, you can usually find her reading, listening to podcasts, or dreaming about her next book.

Learn more about Heidi Stark at her website. Sign up for exclusive content and her newsletter here.

You can also find out more about Heidi and her upcoming books on social media:

Facebook Page

Facebook Group

Instagram

TikTok